Feeling exhausted? Nervous?
seemed to turn in a positive d
throughout the U.S. and the r
rushed a new wave of bigotry, hatred, violence, and fear.

And yet, as this volume materialized, I was repeatedly struck by a nagging sense of…something positive. The call for submissions to *ImageOutWrite Volume 7* was met by an unprecedented deluge of responses. The 31 stories and poems that follow were culled from well over 200 individual works and more than 1200 pages. While the Rochester community still accounts for 10% of submissions, these works came to us from 32 states, 14 countries, and 6 continents. With each new poem or story, I inched toward the realization that these writers were collectively conveying a shared message—one of renewal.

For ImageOut, this is year 26. Now that we're past the 25th anniversary and its celebrations of what the festival has *been*, a new quarter-century is underway. It's time for the writers of the world (script, screen, and otherwise) to answer the question, "What will ImageOut become?"

As a community, we have a lot of these questions to answer.

What will America become?
What will AIDS become?
What will human rights become?
What will our children become?

It's a time of re-becoming for us all, and a time for renewal—of self-discovery, of commitment, of community. Of humanity.

With some battles arguably complete (or, at least, at rest for the moment), we renew our commitment to conquering various specters, some new and some old. As you dig back into the crusades to which you commit your personal energy, focus, and resources, I hope that the stories within energize you by reflecting back the values, experiences, and truths that drive you.

In the words of *ImageOutWrite* founding editor Gregory Gerard, "It is the writer who will bear witness to our collective culture in the years to come." While some may declare our world "post-gay," *ImageOutWrite Volume 7* is a testament to the reality that the LGBTQ+ perspective is as relevant as ever, and our voices still have plenty to say. May it remind you that we're here, we're queer, and you're not alone.

—Jessica Heatly, editor

ImageOutWrite

Volume Seven

Editor:

Jessica Heatly

Reading Panel:

Frances Andreu

Deanna Baker

Elizabeth Bell

Nancy Brown

Ryan DeWolfe

Steven Farrington

Judy Fuller

Gregory Gerard

ISBN 978-0-359-02572-5

Cover graphic design by Jeffrey Cougler.
Cover art, *AIDS Quilt*, by Lola Flash.

Published by ImageOut

Printed in the United States of America
Published September 2018

Table of Contents

This collection is dedicated to an ongoing commitment of speaking truth to power; by sharing our stories, we acknowledge our existence.
#Unite Until #LoveWins

Linda,
the love of
truly good people
holds us together —
keeps us from
falling apart.
Thank you for accepting
me into your family
for loving me.

Eric J. Cook

LET ME ASK YOU SOMETHING

Margaret H. Lange

"When did you know?"
They never fail to ask
"Always"
is the easy answer
but the truth is
more complicated than
two syllables because
the truth is:
knowing is the result
of countless small moments,
invisible
when alone,
but together
build up
thick and obvious
until you can't
ignore them anymore
like too much tree
pollen on a windshield

I knew
when the cheerleaders
visiting my

elementary school made
my second grade
heart wish
I was grown
enough to impress them

I knew
when I went
back to church camp
and thought
my friend
from before wasn't there
the one
who played the viola
and let me
untangle her
hair while
we giggled
in my bunk
but she appeared
preteen paragon
standing in the
doorway
and we were
inseparable again
lost magnets found

I knew

at that sleepover

with girls

who didn't know me

but the one, all

red hair and freckles

and sincere looks and

easy laughs, decided

we would be friends

took my hand

shared a blanket

said she was cold and

leaned her whole self

into me

and that was the

first time I

knew damnation

was worth it

I knew

with that one friend

all summer

while the sun was up

we would

weave traps for

catching blank-faced

farm boys

and flash our breasts
at passing
semi-trucks from
the safety of
her driveway but
at night
I would listen
to her softest breathing
and weep,
with my hand
between my legs
and my eyes
on the moon,
mourning what
we would never
become

I knew
when boy after boy after
man after man after
disappointing man failed
to make me
feel like I
fit anywhere but
the first night
I stepped into the
room with

the three pool tables and
pocket-sized dance floor and
let myself become just
another body
in a crowd of
suspect women
utterly orthodox
perfectly ordinary
my people, my people
my home

I could tell them
about these and
other revelations but
rarely are
straight questions looking
for queer answers

"When did you know?"
Always.

RAINI IS LUCA:
WHEN MY DAUGHTER BECAME MY SON

Shelley Stoehr

A Mother's Perspective on Having a Transgender Child

"I've learned that what matters is whether your child is doing the right things—in school, socially, later on in work—and if they're doing the right things like getting good grades, making good friends, and working hard, then whatever gender they decide to be doesn't really matter."

I was told this by the mother of a child who had been born Amy, changed to Steven in high school, eventually had his name legally changed, and then, after college, decided to go back to being Amy. Push-up bra and everything. Though sometimes, he's still Steven—binders and everything.

Whew. Confusing.

But so, so helpful for me to hear. Necessary. Because my child, my little girl, Raini, had just told me that she was really a boy. He wanted to be called "Luca," and "he" and "my eldest son."

And now he is. But it hasn't been easy, and if it weren't for the helpful advice offered by friends such as Nancy, mother of Amy-Steven-Amy, I wouldn't have been able to make the transition at all.

* * *

It was a Thursday. Eight forty-five in the morning. My daughter, Raini, had left on the bus to middle school—it was the last year she'd be a student at Betsy Ross Arts Middle School in New Haven. My son, Angel, had just gotten on his bus to elementary school. I crossed the street, said good-bye to the other parents, and went back inside my house to begin work. I'm a freelance writer and editor, and work from home.

My office is a desk and shelf combo in the corner of my bedroom. I sat down in that familiar space; in my cat-scratched, swivel chair; kicked off my shoes; and pulled out my laptop. On top lay a folded sheet of paper. Odd. I opened it partway. Across the fold, it read, in blue, glitter-gel ink: "Urgent; read ASAP!"

Clearly from my daughter, Raini. Opening the final fold, I expected a bright blue, "I love you, Mommy!" on the inside. Instead I read:

"Dear Mommy and Daddy,

"I have something to tell you. I'm telling you in this note, because even though I feel like I'll be happier after you know, I'm also going to feel really awkward for a while, and you guys probably will, too...

"...Before I start, I want you to know a few things; I'm not 'experimenting.' I know you guys like to say things like, "It's normal to experiment at this age' but *I'm not experimenting*. This is who I am. Secondly, I want you to know that while I strongly believe this is not a phase, I want it to be okay if it is. Someday, whether it be tomorrow, or 10 years from now, I may feel differently. If it really is a phase, I want you guys to be okay with it."

Okay.

By this point, my mouth had gone dry and my stomach was in knots. I was shaking. What was this? A suicide note? Had she run away? Was she pregnant? I read on:

"As you know, transgender is a term used to describe someone who is seemingly in the wrong body… in short when someone's gender identity doesn't match their biological sex…

"…I've grown up as a girl, but in the past few months, I've felt strange. I've been more comfortable thinking of myself as a boy… with the name, 'Luca.'…

"…I am still the same person. I still like makeup, I still like Hello Kitty, I still want to wear a dress to dinner dance… I still want to do everything I've wanted to do before, but now, as a boy… In the future, maybe you could start referring to me as your son, or using male pronouns. It would make me a lot happier, I know it would. Sorry if this is really overwhelming, and I'm sorry this is such a big change…

"~~Raini~~ Luca Nicholas McCarthy"

Okay. Wow.

I'm almost embarrassed to say, my first reaction was to laugh! I'm not sure what it was that was also going on—car trouble, money trouble, and so forth—but I do know that reading that my little girl was really a boy was too much to bear. It broke me and I laughed. Laughed until I choked.

I showed the letter to a friend, called my mother, called another friend. Waited for Raini to get home from school and my husband, Chris, from work. Cried.

Chris and I tried to be supportive but we didn't have the information to be reasonable at first. We suggested that instead of "Luca," Raini change her name to "Raine," a boy's name. We researched binders and what it meant to be "gender fluid." I talked to a friend who led me to her friend, Nancy (mother of Amy/Steven/Amy.) I emailed and Googled and read and watched videos. Gradually, I came to terms with Raini being a boy.

And when I was ready—a surprisingly short, few days later—I said, "Okay."

Tears rolling over her cheeks, she said, "Forget it. I just want everything to go back to the way it was."

Seriously?

I was a bit perturbed. No, make that pissed off! After all of this, Raini was remaining Raini? What the hell?

But all I said out loud was, "Okay."

And I believed it was.

Then summer came, and Raini got picked up for shoplifting. High school started and she seemed to be doing well, but at the beginning of October, I checked her grades online, and found—to my horror and dismay—that she was failing two of her four academic classes. This was a child who'd excelled in school, a child who, though now failing English, was also writing a novel and read every night. A smart, capable child.

Failing out of high school. With a criminal record.

"What the f—is wrong with our kid?" I asked my husband. Actually, I'm pretty certain that I *yelled* that. Several times.

When I told a friend what was going on with Raini, she said that typically when a kid started acting out the way Raini had, there was something deeper going on. Again, I cried out, "What the f—is wrong with my kid?"

And then, one night about a week later, when I was nagging Raini to clean her room and do her homework, I asked her—"What is going on with you?"

"I know why I'm failing at school," she said, under her breath, with tears brimming in her eyes.

"If you know and you don't tell me, that's pretty mean," I told her.

"I don't want you to overreact."

"I'm already overreacting. Nothing you can tell me will be worse than what I've imagined might be wrong." Which was true—I'd imagined Raini being molested, raped, pregnant, on drugs, alcoholic— never mind that I hadn't any evidence of these things. My mind had been spinning for days.

"I'm still Luca," said my daughter.

"Oh," I said. "Okay."

"Okay, what?"

"Okay, you're Luca. You're a boy. Fine."

"Fine?"

"Yes. Fine. Now get your English grade up."

My husband Chris was out late at a class that night. I was half-asleep when he came home. I woke enough to tell him, "Raini is a boy. Call him Luca. Talk to you tomorrow."

"Okay," he said.

The next day, I sent the following letter to my dearest friends:

"So, my daughter, Raini, has been failing her classes, has been unnecessarily mean and withdrawn… I've been very worried. Then last night somehow something I said triggered her to say, 'I know why my grades have dropped but I can't tell you.'

"Wow.

"I told her that if she knew and wasn't telling me, I thought that was kind of mean, because I haven't been sleeping, I've been struggling to concentrate enough to work, in short, I've been miserable, worrying about her. She said, 'I can't tell you because you're just going to overreact and freak out.' I said, 'I promise, I've already imagined the worst in my mind so anything you tell me is going to be fine.'

"So… she said that she is still 'Luca,' a boy. Her best friends call her 'he' and 'Luca.'

"I was so calm and, frankly, relieved. She was in awe. But I told her that after she wrote me that letter last spring, saying she felt as if she was really a boy and wanted to become a boy, I talked to a lot of people… a mother of a daughter who became a son, a woman who became a man, parents of gay children, and gay friends of both genders. I also researched on the internet and watched a program about teens who are transgender but wear clothes that aren't male or female, just clothes they like—not gender-specific. So by the time Luca came out last night I was already way over my emotional reaction.

"So I'm paying for the binders (breast binders, looks like a sports bra but is more, what's the word? Oppressive? Compressive?), because, I told him, I pay for his underwear, why wouldn't I pay for that? He is feeling overwhelmed by all the people he has to tell and changes he has to make in different areas of his life and I recommended that he make a list and conquer just one item at a time from the list. I said that I can help or advise when it comes to approaching people and also to organizing things/tasks/a to-do list.

"He's making an appointment for us to meet with his guidance counselor at school.

"So that's it. Raini is, for now at least, Luca. I will be calling him 'he' (interestingly, it's been harder for me to use the masculine pronoun than to call him by another name) and referring to him as my son whenever I can remember."

The responses I got back were remarkable:

"Shelley
What an amazing example of an honest, open and trusting relationship between a parent and child.
You are truly blessed to have each other in this journey of life. Oxoxo"

"Love to you all ♡♥♡♥♡♥♡"

"Wow. I really don't know what else to say.... I feel honored to witness such authenticity, love and acceptance. Truly.... xoxo"

"…Congratulations to both you and Raini—sorry, Luca—for getting there."

"I got goosebumps & teary reading this. I already have spoken w/ Shelley. I am just honored to be part of the 'village.'"

* * *

Now, Chris makes jokes, searching for a nickname to replace "Rainbow," Raini's old nickname… "Luc-alive," "Luc-alike."

And it truly is, all okay. I am buying my once-daughter, now eldest son, binders for his chest. I've read that they can damage young breast tissue and so shouldn't be worn for more than 12 hours at a time. Luca informed me that he read eight hours was the maximum. He's on top of this, and I don't have to worry. Much.

"Mommy?" Luca said one night.

"Yes?"

"Thank you."

"For what?"

"For making me so happy. For allowing me to be me."

And so, I stumble over my pronouns and sometimes I cry, but I try my best. My friends are trying as well. It won't happen completely, overnight. But in this moment?

Raini is Luca.

Author's note: This was written soon after my son, Luca, came out as transgender in 2015. It's odd to read it now, and to remember those days when we struggled to understand him. It's been years now since I've heard or read the name, Raini. For new "trans-parents," I offer this: after a while, gender stops being such a huge concern, and in fact, your teen resumes being just your child, with normal teenaged concerns. Hang in there! It's not as hard as it looks in the beginning. One day, *you'll* be the relaxed and helpful mom or dad on the other end of the phone.

A feature-length documentary about Ren and Luca, called *Little Miss Westie,* will be released in October of this year (2018).

OTHER

Reilly Hirst

You name me a name that isn't mine.

That I won't own today.

That isn't for reclaiming.

I won't stand in the parking space you gave me for it.

I won't stand nicely and complacently to the side. I stand where I am. I stand next to you beside you and inside of you.

Declaring a new nation. Declaring a new world with boundaries. Outside. Outside of all of us. Because we all get to be who we are.

Even you. Even you who rips and burn our flags. Paints swastikas on walls. Grabs women. Kills the other as each time you kill more of yourself. Each injury is a rip in your own soul, your own knowledge.

This is our world.
I won't take you prisoner because we all get to be free.

I won't take you prisoner.

You have already done that.

Shackled yourself to a lie, to a smaller version of what you could be.

To a smaller world.

If you're in chains, it's not me who put you there.

Look in the mirror and decide when you will be free. When you will let your hate release you

When you know your own enemy Is in the mirror, in your soul

And not in my life. You are your persecuter, your own jailer.

Tell the world when you finally know your truth.

When you finally find the key the last prisoners might finally be free.

WAS GONE

Cirrus Julian

Lori is calling to make sure I took my medicines earlier. The clinic has me taking three huge, stick-in-your-throat tablets every morning. I like to watch myself swallowing in the mirror so I know I'm really doing it. Then I'll bare my teeth to see if they're still yellowish.

There are no mirrors in my kitchen yet. That's where I am now, cradling the phone between my shoulder and cheek so I can keep scrubbing dishes while I talk. "Yeah. Of course."

"Oh." Surprised. She was ready to lecture me. She always is. On the phone, anyway. She didn't say anything to me when I was at the clinic earlier. She tries again. "You're really supposed to stay in the office for at least thirty minutes after your injections."

"I did." I actually waited forty. Price says forty and he knows a little more than Lori and the other nurses. "I'm fine. No problems."

Nurses are supposed to make sure I've had my pills before they give me the shots. Lori sighs heavily into the receiver. "Alright. Well. If you're sure." She pauses. "We'll see you on Thursday, dear." She hangs up before I can say anything else.

I drain the sink. I lean over the water and watch the blurry image of my face swirl and get sucked down with all the little bits of old food and greasy bubbles, leaving a patchier reflection in the dirty metal. I step back and lift my arms, feeling the sting where she stuck me with two big needles in each. It's important that Lori makes sure I've had my pills before I get shots because without the pills the shots don't work.

Or. Wait. Without the shots the pills don't work. One or the other. It's in a notebook somewhere.

A blue Post-it on the fridge tells me I should shower today. I peel the green one off the microwave because it says *Do the dishes!* with a few flowers scribbled on the bottom. I crumple it and stuff it in my pocket. I walk to the bathroom, and on the way another blue note says *Remember to listen* with a smiley face, so I close my eyes and listen to how the old floorboards creak under me. I count the steps I take. Thirteen. I'm here. Fourteen. Fifteen.

It's only been six months. No one thought the medicine would work this quick. Price said a year. Price looks really friendly when there's other people around. He's got a gap between his front teeth and big glasses that look like they weigh a ton. He smiles a lot. But on the first day of treatment he stopped smiling when he took me into another room and sat me down and explained everything to me again, even though I read it all in emails four or five times. He gave me this laminated sheet of paper that had the exact same words as one of the emails. I kept glancing down at it. *By attempting to alter how the human form is perceived by...such that a specific face...body...by extension...made completely...impossible to remember.*

He said he didn't know how long it would take before everyone forgot but probably at least a year and he didn't know if I would forget too because none of the mice had forgotten what they looked like but I might and he said some other things and then he said, *Are you sure?*

When I told my friends about Price they didn't get as far as *are you sure*. I thought they would understand. They were like me, all of us constantly trying to look different or right, pushing at our bodies or

20

pulling something, draping our clothes just right and praying stupidly to be seen like we want to, or like we see ourselves when we're looking right or not looking at all. We gathered together over time, finding solace in hearing our real names with regularity over strong-brewed tea and Super Smash Bros. We'd talk about how we got seen or didn't. We'd talk about anything, *anything* else. Rhea's basement was our refuge.

But we still hurt. I didn't tell anyone that I liked being alone because I didn't have to hear my voice. I didn't have to tell anyone. A lot of us felt that way. I would wear a binder for too long for too many days until it stretched out so much it didn't work anymore, the thick elastic slackening more every time I dragged it down around me to crush my breasts flat. My ribs throbbed like they were bruised, even though they never looked any more purple in the mirror. But I felt wrong if I didn't. I tried to make my voice low and my throat hurt a lot. I was so, so tired. I thought my friends were tired, too. Jack was always uncomfortable because he sits kind of funny around the balled-up wool sock he fidgets into his underwear every morning. I know his throat hurts too. Ari kept saying they wanted people to stop staring at their thighs. They only wore black jeans and spread their hands across their lap to make them look smaller. I wasn't the only one who bound for too long, either. Rhea gave great back rubs and that wasn't enough.

We were all trying to look like something else, desperate, like bailing water out of a sinking ship. Damage control, making up for our bodies. I couldn't do it anymore. I'd come home and stand in front of the single mirror I had then, poring over my body, trying to pick out exactly what had warranted the woman pushing around me on the sidewalk to name me *Excuse me, ma'am.* I'd trace with my hands like knives. If I could just change this, this thing, was it my *hips* or some*thing*? Or everything?

At night I'd run through my impossible solution, the stupid one that helped me get to some kind of fitful sleep. I thought it might get better if we didn't have to be seen at all. Invisibility isn't real. But it would help, right? If I couldn't be seen, I couldn't be seen wrong. That was the whole thing. Then I'd wake up and be seen and named wrong and I'd look away because if I couldn't see anyone I couldn't watch them see.

And it wasn't real. But then Miriam sent me an ad Price's lab was posting around, following the link with seven question marks, waiting for me to respond with the expected incredulity. Because *why would anyone do an experiment like this* or some*thing*. She meant it as a joke when she said one of us should try it.

We all hung out at Rhea's place and I pulled it up on my phone screen and passed it around and someone laughed. I told them I was going to do it and no one laughed anymore.

Everyone was worried and then they got angry really fast. I got angry back because I thought, *I thought they would understand* and *what about this makes me stupid* and *I would be paid so can you really blame me* and *I was practically fucking invisible anyway* and Rhea led me outside by the arm but they just tried to say everything everyone else said in a quieter voice so I walked home without saying anything else.

On the first day of my treatment a few weeks later I told Price *yes* and he didn't get angry. He nodded and pushed some pieces of paper across the table so I could tell him I was sure again. Then he smiled weird and said *Okay. Let's start.*

A yellow note on the shower wall where the water can't get it says I have to go to the store today. I hate going to the store so I take a really long shower. When I get out I look in the mirror for a long time. I memorize. I look feminine. Or I don't. I could never decide unless someone told me, you know? Sometimes I feel like I can't see myself at all, you know? Like I'm looking too close and everything's all blurry. But that's not all just the medicine. It's always been like that.

I wear bright colors today. There are notes by the door reminding me to put on shoes and gloves and a coat. I do those things and walk to Jewel Osco. I'm still feeling a little sick from the shots. Or the pills. I know by now I won't feel better until the evening. Sometimes I don't feel better at all.

I'm dizzy when I get to the store. I'm supposed to record every interaction I have with everyone while I'm here, but the nurses haven't asked for a report in a week or month. I have a meeting with Price on Thursday. I'll just tell him then if I remember.

I was never great at eating. It's the anxiety, maybe, or the misguided thrift. I'd buy cheap produce and watch a lot of it turn funny colors and get squishy. Sometimes I'd be ravenous. Sometimes most things tasted like sandpaper and all I could eat with any degree of consistency was grapefruits and cheese on saltines. Sometimes Miriam would come over and make me a peanut-butter-and-honey sandwich with all the crusts cut off. She'd watch me pull it apart and eat a quarter-sized chunk at a time. She'd complain the whole time and laugh. She wasn't worried.

Price seems worried or maybe just annoyed. I told him I didn't have as many sandwiches anymore because Miriam stopped talking to me a few weeks after the trial started. He didn't think that was funny. The last time Miriam came over she asked what happened to my face and I told her nothing and she told me to stop lying and then she cried and then she gathered her things really slowly, *goddamnit, goddamnit* she said, and then she was gone.

I get prepared meals delivered now. The store's for *research*. Which no one except Price remembers to ask about. The store's for going outside.

I put four grapefruits in a basket. I ask an employee where I can find the saltines. "Aisle four," he says, smiling at me. He turns away and looks confused for a second. I tap him on the shoulder and ask him again. "Aisle four," he says with a smile "Someone else *just* asked me that," he says to himself, and then to me, "You can follow…" He turns away and I watch him forget again.

I know the cashier. She's been working here as long as I've lived here. Before the medicine she would ask me how I was doing at work and whether I had been getting enough sleep while she weighed my produce. Now she takes my groceries and smiles and doesn't say anything. She looks up and her mouth twitches up blankly. "You find everything okay today?"

She doesn't recognize me and won't. If I tell her who I am she'll look away and think someone told her a story once, or that she just remembered someone from a while ago. She looks up again and seems confused when she sees me, or doesn't. "Your total is eight-thirty-four."

I go home and eat saltines, sucking at the corners until they rot away in my mouth. I sit in front of the TV with my box of Post-its and make notes for tomorrow, watching the neon paper wash out in the bluish glow of nighttime murder mysteries. I make more than usual, in case tomorrow is the day I forget what I haven't.

*   *   *

I have three full-length mirrors now. A couple weeks ago, Price started fidgeting in his chair a lot and then he told me I needed to spend some time every day memorizing what I look like. He bought two of the mirrors for me so I do what he says.

Brown eyes. *Rabo.* I'm not very tall. *Julian.* My teeth are straight, *River,* thanks to the orthodontural hell I endured as a pre-teen. I never told the doctor if my teeth hurt. *Charlie.*

No one calls me by name anymore. Price calls me by my last name. That's why I call him by his. Not that I remember his first. Doctor? Anyway, it's just me now and I can't get a name to stick. *Eddy. Leon. Al.* Nothing.

At the clinic today, Price said I've gained some weight. He sounded nervous and relieved. He's always worried I'll become underweight. I've always been skinny, but I guess he's a real doctor and so he gets to worry about things like that. I lift my arms over my head. I'm half-naked like I always am in private summertime so I get a good look at my torso. I screw up my face when I make out the shape of it, but relax again. My skin's so pale it's almost bright and my ribs stick out funny. My breasts push out more when I lower my arms and I flinch again. It's always been like that.

There's a note on the wall. *Did you eat breakfast?* It's got a crudely drawn flower with a big smile. When I started writing notes, I decided I would write them like they're for someone else. They come out nicer that way.

Or I try to write them like Rhea writes. Sometimes Rhea would write me notes like this but nicer, somehow. Rhea's much nicer than I am. They remembered my address, came by a month ago. They didn't look at me much but they told me they'd been worried. Then they looked at me for a long time. I told them they could call me, it's easier to talk over the phone. They looked at the ground and I told them again. They promised they would and didn't ask for my new phone number.

How skinny am I? Do I look sick or naturally thin? I lift my arms over my head and look in the mirror. My ribs stick out funny. *Wren.* My eyes are brown. *Caleb.*

* * *

"You could do with more exercise. I know we haven't had the best system for that, but you could be getting out more. We're gonna try another chart. You'll just turn it in to me."

Price is scribbling something on a memo pad. He has notes all over his monitor and desk, one on his wrist. He's more prepared than most. It's important that he remembers he's talking to me. He's good about that. Is that his *bedside manner?* Is he my doctor?

Price doesn't look like a doctor. He doesn't look like a crazy scientist, or what you think a crazy scientist who makes people sort of gone looks like. He wears a lot of big blue button-downs from Goodwill and khakis. He's tall and he slouches a lot to look smaller. He doesn't feel very far away at all.

26

He looks up at me, fidgeting with his glasses and focusing on my face. I can tell he's having a hard time keeping his eyes still. People's gazes tend to kind of slip off of me. I think of it like a raindrop rolling off a sloped roof. Price doesn't think that's funny. He doesn't like it when I make jokes and he won't tell me why and I know anyway. I want to remind him that this was my choice. I don't think he gives me that much credit. "Is that okay? Does that work for you?"

He always sounds like he's sorry. I'm not any sorrier now than I was before I signed up. Different sorry, maybe. I think it's okay. "I can do that, yeah." I wince at my voice and wonder if he can notice that.

He smiles with his mouth shut and uneasy. "Excellent, thank you."

I look forward to the check-ins with Price. I'm smiling a little when I leave his office. Then a nurse takes me back and I stop smiling.

I don't like it when Sharon is the one to give me shots. She was really nice in the beginning. She doesn't say anything to me anymore. She swabs down my arms and I glare up at her. I wonder if I'm really angry or if I just want to remember what it feels like to look angry. "Do you remember me?"

She looks up and smiles and then she goes to prepare the injections and forgets. The cabinet above her is covered in big notes that remind her I'm here.

I clear my throat. "I have a high-pitched voice and dark brown eyes. My hair is short and straight and brown. I'm five feet and four inches tall. I have long fingers."

I hiss when she sticks me with the first needle. I talk after the second shot. "I have a big nose and it's lumpy. I have straight teeth and freckles on my nose."

She moves to the other arm. "I wear mostly t-shirts. I breathe kind of shallow. I'm skinny. You can see my ribs when I'm naked."

I wait my forty minutes. I don't do anything. I count the floor tiles even though I did that the first day and the number hasn't changed. "I bite my nails," I tell Sharon on the way out.

The sun's out and painfully bright light shoots up from the sidewalk and off the cars in the clinic parking lot. I look down at my hands. I have long fingers. I have fingers. If I put my hand next to someone else's hand, could I still pick it out?

I take a really long way home so that my feet hurt, I think. I'm sitting on the floor, just inside, peeling off my socks to look at my feet and see if they look any different when they're sore.

A week later I walk into a table and bruise my hip. I look at it in the mirror for thirty minutes. That looks different.

Three days after that Price asks me a question and it takes me twenty-three seconds to remember how to move my mouth and respond. He writes something on a Post-it and sticks it on his computer without looking at me.

The next day I remember that and I feel scared. At night someone delivers lasagna and vegetables in two cold foil containers and I stare at his hands for a long time because they look silver. "Your hands look silver," I say. He's gone. "My hands don't look silver," I say. Then I hold my fingers up to the porchlight. "My hands."

I go upstairs that night or the next morning, I think. I take everything off quickly and look in the mirror. I see my eyes, I think. My shoulders. I lift my arms. I see my ribs. My teeth, I think. My hair. My arms are lifted and that makes my ribs stick out. I see my ribs. My eyes. My teeth. My arms are lifted.

U'LL FEEL ME ALL AROUND U

Marissa Layne Johnson

i think about dying a lot

but only cuz I'm looking for the endings

to all my losses

some things outlive our bodies

like love & regret & the space

we leave behind with nothing but our smell

u ever scream and make no sound

u ever think this is it

and still wake up w/ the sun coming

through ur blinds, u ever

hold on for too long

or laugh harder than everyone else

sometimes i shower just

to be naked, sometimes

i disagree just to be heard, sometimes

i believe it when they say

they love me. i like sad songs

and girls who don't say my name and

rainy days, how they all got me wet and

breathing through my mouth, desperate like

somewhere between hungry and drowning
i dance like i'm becoming the air and
love like i already am, at least i think
this is how we keep on living, anyway

ORIGINAL SIN

Stacey Darlington

Instead of getting dressed, I lay on my bed staring at the ceiling fan, not wanting to move. I had butterflies in my stomach about the possibilities the night could bring. Not actual butterflies, you know, but that sensation. I was nervous with her on the bed beside me. I giggled at the butterfly thing because being next to her made me giddy. Three years had passed since I'd held her in my arms. My beautiful Siren neglected because just seeing her was an aching reminder of our unattainable dream. Would she still feel the same to me?

I closed my eyes, smiling at the memory of how our bodies fit together. Our perfect rhythm. She had always surrendered to my touch, lyrically vocal to the tempo of my deft fingers. Did I still possess the same passion in my hands necessary to evoke her wails and screams? Worse yet, could I perform at all?

I reached over and stroked her silky neck. The sensation made me shiver and my years of missing her made me bold. I pulled her close, easing her into position. I caressed her curves, instantly aroused by the weight of her on top of me. Her exotic scent drove me wild. I made a few adjustments and when she was properly tuned, I sat up and began to play. Even without an amplifier, she sounded great. *She* was my cherry red Fender Stratocaster.

After running some scales and scratching out a few chords, I polished her up and tucked her back into her case. Now I was ready to get dressed. It would be our first gig since we'd gone our separate ways three years ago. All-female bands were always in fashion and I knew Jazz would make sure that we were playing to a packed house. I would have preferred to have at least one practice first, but Jazz thought that winging it would be part of the fun. Besides, it wasn't geographically feasible.

Feeling confident that I still had my guitar chops, I checked my reflection to see if I still had *it*. Thanks to my healthy lifestyle and Northern Italian roots, I still looked good. I wasn't in my twenties anymore but I'd managed to hold off the ravages of time. I'm a blonde with green eyes, if that detail is important to you.

I never was one to play at the edge of the stage; I preferred to perform from the shadows. I was the songwriter in the group and the lyrics told my stories. That was good enough. Besides, Jazz was the main event and eclipsed us all when she entered any room.

Jasmine Cole, Jazz to her fans, considered herself the axis on which the world turned. She had good reason for the massive ego. With her sultry Mediterranean looks and smoky voice, she was a crowd-pleaser on and off stage. Heavily pursued by both men and women, Jazz preferring the latter, she effortlessly pandered to her adoring fans, keeping them at bay and close at the same time. Everyone believed they had a chance at Jazz. Her perfect pout of a mouth and her innocent doe eyes made her a real living doll. Her stature allowed her to command any room and don't let me get started on her body!

Her sex appeal was only for public consumption; in private, she was intellectual, with a mind as vast and luminous as the night sky. Only I knew the real her, how she disliked to be objectified and how it was all part of the game. When we met, she had just reached legal drinking age.

I thought it was cute that she only sipped liqueur. It didn't take long for her to acquire a taste for martinis and wine. Lots of martinis and wine.

Over time, I watched, helplessly, as the two parts of her began to meld together. Her blooming ego became a cloying flower. Soon I could barely breathe. The hardest thing I have ever done was to turn my back on my muse and my music, but our lives were spinning out of control. My desire to create waned in the wake of her rising storm. I had to leave to save myself. In case you haven't guessed, Jazz is my ex.

Mr. Velvet, my cat, slunk like a tiny panther from his place on top of the fridge. He sat on top of my guitar case and fixed me with his ocher eyes.

"Can you manage one night without me?" I asked, scooping him into my arms. "Sara will be by to check on you later."

He stared at me adoringly and I covered his face in kisses until he squirmed for release.

"That should hold you until I return."

He ignored me and groomed his paw.

I shouldered my overnight bag, grabbed my guitar case, and headed out the door. In my car, I double-checked my make-up in the rearview mirror, surprised by my scowl. I plucked a piece of Mr. Velvet's hair from my mouth and reapplied my lipstick. Jazz had insisted that we turn the gig into a reunion and had gotten us a block of rooms at the beach resort where we were playing. Touted as the largest gay complex in central Florida, Jazz insisted it would be crawling with luscious lesbians. I giggled at the thought of lesbians swarming like ants, busy with the task of feeding their queen. There would be slim pickings for us drones with Jazz at the center of the mound. That was fine by me. I had been single since our break-up and planned to stay that way. Forever.

Luckily, for me it was just a short drive to the gig; the rest of the girls would be coming from different parts of the state and beyond. I'll admit I was excited. Having my guitar in my hands again had evoked a feeling of euphoria like no drug in the world. Secretly, I hoped Jazz had gotten fat. I fed our CD into the slot and turned it up, memorizing my guitar riffs. Thankfully, I was the first of our foursome to arrive at the hotel.

I checked into my room, pleased at the king-sized bed and other lavish furnishings. The days of the four of us piling into one room were well behind me. I liked my own space. I peeled off the comforter and replaced it with one I had brought from home. I immediately hung my clothes in the closet, making sure they would be wrinkle-free for my performance. I set up my toiletries on the bathroom counter and smelled the bath towels for freshness.

The mini bar tempted me, but I never drink before I play. I checked my watch. We wouldn't be hitting the stage for four more hours and rules were made to be broken, besides, I was nervous. One little drink couldn't hurt. I grabbed some ice from the machine in the hall and made myself a cocktail. I took my drink to the balcony and settled into a chair. It was a rare day in Florida, one we northern transplants lived for, mid-seventies, low humidity and an early sunset. The low humidity part was good for my crazy mane of hair.

I had specifically asked for a beachfront room and the view was spectacular. Umbrellas and sunbathers decorated the white sand making me think of sprinkles on an ice cream cone. The way the sun dazzled on the water made me breathless. I rushed into my room and grabbed my Nikon from my overnight bag. I focused the camera and panned the coastline, looking for the perfect shot.

I focused briefly on a woman wearing a large hat, reading. Curious, I zoomed into see what book held her in such rapt attention. Startling me, the woman turned and looked directly into the camera. My nervous finger hit the button and snapped her picture by mistake. She peered directly into the lens. I took the next shot on purpose. She was the most stunning woman I'd ever seen. I noted that she wisely wore the hat to protect her fair, freckled skin. Her eyes were a startling shade of blue. She gave me a playful grin, replaced her sunglasses, and returned to her book.

Shaking, I grabbed my drink and went back inside, drawing the blinds behind me. I wasn't some creepy voyeur! Mortified at the thought, I perched on the edge of the bed and reviewed the pictures anyway. Her crystal blue eyes held me captive. Her gaze was both playful and bold. I zoomed in and studied the angle of her face, the sparkle of her teeth, her perfect nose. Further inspection revealed that the book she held was *Synchronicity and the Paranormal.* I also enjoyed Carl Jung and owned the same book!

A loud knock on my door brought me back to reality.

"Open up, Sinclair! It's me!" Lala squealed through the door, banging with two fists. "Let me get a handful of those titties!"

Instinctively, I crossed my arms over my chest and muttered, "Oh Jesus."

On the other side of the door stood our bass player, LuAnn Abernathy, otherwise known as Lala. She was a self-professed Georgia peach with a heavy southern accent and a Colgate smile.

"Come on, Sweetums, I won't grab your bodacious boobies, just open the door!"

I went to the door and yanked it open. "Lala!"

She burst into the room and wrapped me in a hug. "Oh, I've missed you, girl," she growled in my ear. Before she released me, Lala grabbed my rear end with two hands and squeezed.

I squirmed from her embrace, fully understanding how Mr. Velvet felt as the victim of my passion.

"Sinclair Stevens, you look fabulous," Lala beamed. "I've missed you. And, I've missed these!" She grasped both of my breasts and made a honking sound.

I took her hands in mine and stared at her gravely. "Lala that is seriously the most sex I've had in three years."

She tossed her head back and laughed. "Well, don't go fallin' in love, now. Ya know I'm a married woman." She flashed me her diamond ring and her winning smile. "Not that you cared enough to come." With that, her smile faded and I saw the hurt in her eyes.

"I'm sorry," I said. "I wanted to, I really did. I had a deadline."

"I know you did, Sin. However, we both know you also didn't want to run into Jazz. Anyway, that's yesterday, let's focus on today."

I watched her rummage through the mini bar, wondering if we should lock it up before Jazz arrived and looted it. Lala brought out a tiny bottle of Chardonnay. She unscrewed the cap and raised the bottle.

Taking my drink, I touched it to hers and said, "A toast to you and Nancy, may your love last forever," True, it was lame but I was trying.

"No," Lala said. "This toast is to the return of Original Sin."

Lala and I sat in a corner of the balcony, me with my back to the beach for fear I would spy the woman again. Worse yet, that she would see me. I had left my hotel door ajar for when the others arrived. Lala sipped her second wine and I nursed my same drink.

"I'm glad you're still playing," I lied to Lala. The truth was, I had suffered a sting of jealousy when I'd found out she had formed another band. The tension between us was not simply because I had not attended her wedding. Lala harbored a grudge that I had refused to allow her to use our original songs in her current project.

She shrugged. "Just cover songs; you know nobody in the band can write." She glared at me pointedly.

"At least you're the lead vocalist now and you're making money doing something you love," I said, swirling the ice in my glass, avoiding her eyes.

"You know I don't need the money," Lala drawled, dropping me a wink. "But, you know me, Sin, without music in my life I will wither and die! Give me those songs, Sin!"

I giggled at the drama in her voice. "Come on, I'll let you grab my boobs if you just chill on the subject."

Lala stomped her foot. "Come on, Sinclair! You're not using the songs. I co-wrote on some. Let me use them, they're too good to waste."

"I will not let anyone else sing them. The answer is still no."

"Will your obsession with Jazz ever end?" She reached over and grabbed one of my breasts in consolation.

I swatted her hand. "It's not about Jazz. The songs are my babies, born of my experience and, well, mostly of my pain. It was a hard labor."

"You're a laborious pain," Lala sulked. "Jazz isn't the only singer in the world! I know you think she shits rubies and emeralds, but she's not the only one who can sing."

"Actually, I shit diamonds."

We both turned to see Jazz towering above us wearing her usual smirk, low-cut shirt and a pair of very expensive-looking boots. Seeing her felt like a punch in the gut. Lala stammered out a greeting, giving me a chance to compose myself.

"Jazz! Jazzy Jazz, I know you perspire pearls and your tears are made of sugar." She hugged Jazz around the waist. I noticed that Jazz patted Lala's head like a pet.

"Still jealous, I see," Jazz said, pulling away.

"And so?" Lala said, with a flip of her curls. "At least I can admit the way I feel." The last line she directed at me.

I rose to greet Jazz. We locked eyes for a moment and I traveled back to the first time we met, searching her face for that innocence. I guess I stared too long and my eyes drifted to her abundant cleavage because in the distance I heard Jazz say, "See something you like?"

"What?"

"You're staring, see something you like?" Jazz repeated.

"Uh, yeah nice boobs, oh I mean boots. I like your boots. They're nice."

"Oh, Jesus H. Christ, get a room," Lala muttered, rolling her eyes as she shoved past Jazz and disappeared behind the blinds.

Jazz played with her necklace and smiled. "Yeah, thanks. I get a ton of compliments. On. My. Boots."

"I'm sure you do."

"Looks like Lala is still jealous as fuck," Jazz said, frowning.

"She loves you, you know that," I said.

"*She* does?" Jazz grinned.

"Doesn't everyone?" I gave Jazz a brief hug and left her alone on the balcony.

"Order up some room service, Sin, you know what I want," Jazz called. "I think you got the best room! We're hanging in here after the show."

It's true, some things never change. I tried not to sigh, wondering why I had agreed to this. I suppose because the years had dimmed the memories of our emotional disharmony off stage. On stage, the chemistry was better than the best sex I've ever had, but behind the scenes, we simply didn't fit. And I was not going to host an after-party in my room!

I found Lala supine on the bed, shoeless, chatting on her cell phone with her wife. I picked up the house phone and ordered a martini and shrimp cocktail for Jazz. I ordered seared tuna for myself and for Lala. I also got a burger and fries for Mags.

I sat down on the bed next to Lala, who repositioned herself with her feet on my lap.

"Sin, please, I need your magic hands. My dogs are aching. Nancy said she read your latest book and loved it, by the way," Lala said.

At least Lala's feet were clean and cute. "Tell her thank you," I said as I began the foot massage that would hail Jazz from the balcony. "Ask her to kindly leave me a review, and I cannot stress the word 'kind' enough here. Her last one wasn't."

"She said she already did and gave you five stars!" Lala sang. "She said she only gave you three on the other one because it didn't have enough sex in it. Dear God, Sin! How the hell are you still single with those enchanted hands?" Lala emphasized her statement with an orgasmic moan.

Jazz peered inside from the patio, grinning. "I'm next."

"I have to save my hands for later," I told her. "Your food and drink should be arriving soon, my queen."

"Mama like," Jazz said.

"Come in here with us," Lala called to Jazz.

"Hold on, I have my eyes on a hot blonde on the beach. I don't care for her hat, and she's a reader. Boring! But damn she's gorgeous. I hope she's here for the show."

"Ouch, easy, Sinclair, that hurt!" Lala whined when I squeezed too hard.

I mumbled, "Sorry."

"Shit, she's leaving. Damn, she's got some long, sexy legs," Jazz said, drawing the blinds and dropping into a chair across from the bed.

"Aren't you seeing someone, Jazz, a lawyer lady?" Lala asked, leaning up on her elbow.

Jazz looked at me as if to gauge my reaction. I ignored her look.

"Yes, she's a well-established defense attorney, not just some lawyer lady," Jazz stated. "So what?"

"A healthy relationship requires devotion and commitment," Lala drawled, staring at her wedding ring with adoration. "You should honor your union and not leer after other women. That's all I'm saying."

"I wasn't leering, I was admiring. I'm not a man for fuck's sake," Jazz argued. "I enjoy looking at beautiful things."

I felt her eyes on me but refused to return her gaze. Luckily, Mags arrived.

Lala leapt from the bed to greet her, almost knocking me over in her haste. "Mags McGee, long time no see! See what I did there?" She swatted Mags' behind and pulled her into the room by her hand. It was an easy task because Mags was tiny. Barely five feet tall and a hundred pounds but played the drums as if she had twenty hands and feet. She flipped her shaggy red bangs off her face to reveal her melted eye make-up and blood-shot eyes.

"What's wrong, Mags?" I asked, rushing to hug her. "Did something happen?"

Mags dropped her purse on the floor and bawled, "I ran over a squirrel! I think I killed it."

Jazz didn't bother to get up from her chair as she offered her opinion, "Squirrels are indecisive assholes. It's not your fault."

I glared at her and Jazz simply shrugged and said, "It's true."

I grabbed a beer from the mini bar and thrust it into Mags' hand. "Do you think a beer and a burger will help?"

Mags hugged me with her free arm and said, "Yeah, a little, maybe." She upended the beer and drained it like a frat boy. She belched and crushed the can. I grabbed the can from her before she could attempt to toss it into a nearby waste pail. I didn't need beer juice staining the carpet.

Lala and I hugged Mags like a sandwich until the food arrived. "Poor squirrel," Mags cried. "Poor little guy didn't deserve to die."

"I ran over a rabbit once," Jazz began.

"On purpose?" I growled, interrupting her.

"Funny girl," Jazz said. She rose from her seat and tipped the room service girl, then wheeled the cart over to us. She took her martini back to the chair.

I used a napkin to wipe Mags' mascara-smeared face. "Come on, doll, eat. You'll feel better."

"Can I have another beer?" Mags asked, her voice shaking,

I tried not to sigh. Instead, I bit my lip and got her another one.

"Okay, but drink slowly, please. All of you," I said, looking at Jazz. "I'm not so much as taking my guitar out of the case tonight if any of you get drunk before the show. I mean it."

Jazz sipped her drink, scowling. "This thing isn't even cold. You know I like a sheer of ice on the top of my martinis and three olives not two. Three! Is this even Grey Goose? Get room service back here."

"No, I'll go down to the bar myself," I said, fairly bolting from the room. I needed to get out of there.

"And make sure…" Jazz called after me.

"Yeah, yeah, three olives and a sheer of ice. I'll be back in a bit."

I stabbed at the elevator button, pacing, staring at the light above the door. It had taken less than thirty minutes of being in their company and I was already in a full-blown panic. If my things weren't back in the

44

room, I might have actually gotten in my car and sped for the safety of home. I'll say it again; some things never change.

The elevator opened and, what a blessing, it was empty. I got in and pressed the button for the first floor. I studied the poster on the wall, squinting at the picture. It was an old band photo, but we mostly still looked the same. Lala's hair was a few inches shorter now and Mags' hair was a more shocking shade of red then. Jazz looked the same, her full lips and her dreamy, dark eyes, her ubiquitous cleavage.

I heard myself emit a groan and caught a reflection of my grimace in the elevator mirror. Maybe Lala was right. It was possible I had lingering feelings for Jazz.

I read the poster: *The Sunstate Resort is proud to host a command performance by all-female rock band, Original Sin. Featuring Jazz on lead vocals. Lala Abernathy on bass guitar and backup vocals. Sinclair Stevens on rhythm and lead guitar. Mags McGee on drums. Showtime 8 pm.*

I was locked in. Showtime at eight. That didn't give the four of us much time to drop the drama and get cohesive. I stepped out of the elevator and quickly found the lounge. Without looking around, I stepped up to the bar and ordered Jazz's drink from an overzealous bartender.

"It's you!" he said, pointing a finger at me. "From the band," he stammered, pointing the same finger at the poster behind the bar.

I exhaled slowly and forced a smile. "Yep, that's me. Can I get an ice cold Grey Goose martini with three olives, please?"

"Hell yes, you can!" He poured the drink and rattled the martini shaker above his head like a maraca. "Are you single? Oh my God, my best friend, Kate, would eat you alive!"

"Why? Is she a zombie?" I joked.

He squealed with laughter. "*And* you're funny! You should let me set you up with her! I'll call her right now. She is adorable, super girly and she loves musicians. So? Are you single?"

"No," I lied. "She sounds amazing but I'm not available."

He winked at me. "Yeah, you musician types like to play the field, huh?"

I guess he noticed me gaping at the blonde from the beach, who sat a mere few feet from me. My heart sank as the woman laughed with the man beside her brushing his arm with the back of her hand. She was even more breathtaking close up. Perhaps feeling my eyes on her, she glanced over at me and gave me a friendly smile.

I gave her what I hoped was a smile and turned my attention back to the bartender. "I'm not the stereotypical musician-type," I told him as I paid for the martini. "I'm more of an out-fielder."

"Fair enough," the bartender said, beaming at his generous tip. "I don't think that one's gay, anyway. Pretty, though. I've never seen her here before."

"Yeah, she's pretty," I agreed, trying not to look her way again. Pretty straight. I wondered if it was possible that she'd recognized me as the salacious voyeur spying on her from the third-floor balcony.

"My name is Eric," the bartender said. "I'll be working the outside bar during your show tonight. I can't wait!"

"Great to meet you, Eric," I said, pausing to take a sip of Jazz's drink. "You make a perfect martini, sir. My name is…"

"Sinclair Stevens! I know!" he squealed, like a teenager at a Justin Bieber concert.

This time I felt *her* eyes on me, drawn by Eric's excited shriek.

She turned fully in her chair and appraised me with her bright eyes. She studied my face as if she recognized me from somewhere but couldn't quite place me. I wheeled around and exited before she could.

Flustered by her curious look, I drank half of Jazz's martini on the elevator ride back to my room. And, I ate one of the olives.

Upon my return, I found the group sitting on the floor, practicing. Mags had turned over a garbage can and now used it like a drum. Lala layered perfect alto harmonies with Jazz's soprano. It was so good I got chills and temporarily forgot about the blonde.

"Amazing!" I said, handing Jazz her drink.

"Hey! What happened to my martini?" Jazz asked, peering into the glass.

"I got thirsty," I told her as I rooted through my bag and pulled out our set list. I handed them each a copy. "Okay, I thought we could start with 'Black Widow,' you know because it's so powerful and the harmonies are fantastic…"

Jazz crumpled up the paper and flung it at my head. "No."

"No, what?" I asked, picking up the paper. "You don't want to start with that song?"

"No set list," Jazz replied, getting up. "I said we are winging it and I mean all the way. So, be on your toes, bitches. I'll call a song and that's the one we play."

"Cool!" Mags said, jumping up and grabbing her bag. "I need to go set up my kit. Jazz, I love that idea. Wing, wing winging it!"

I replaced the waste pail in its original place and smoothed the comforter on my bed. "Cool? No, that's not cool, we need order, we need structure and discipline."

"*You* need order and discipline," Jazz said, touching her finger to the tip of my nose. "Loosen your belt for once, Sinclair, let yourself breathe a little."

Jazz downed what remained of her drink and strolled to the door. "See you on stage, ladies."

After Jazz left, I stared at Lala and Mags. "Really?" I asked. "Really? No set list? This is okay with you?"

"I like it," Mags said with a shrug. "It will be fun."

"Fun?" I asked, turning to Lala. "Fun?"

"Come on, Sin, it's just one itty-bitty show. Big deal. Just go with it. It will be over before you know it and you can get back to your pristine, controlled environment." She slapped my rear end on her way out. "You might be able to get around better without that stick up your ass, darlin'. See you onstage, Sweeeetummms."

I stared at the door long after she was gone. Was I that rigid and uptight? I loosened my belt a notch.

"I don't have a stick up my ass," I muttered, refastening my belt.

I ate the remaining pieces of tuna and then wheeled the room service cart outside.

I went to the closet and laid my clothes on the bed. I stood back, pleased that everything was perfectly matched, coordinated, and accessorized. Maybe I was a little controlling. A little. However, chaos doesn't sit well with me. That's why things hadn't worked with Jazz.

Lala was wrong. It wasn't one itty-bitty show! There had to be over five hundred people thronging through the resort. I gripped my guitar case and plowed my way through the crowd. Dance music boomed from the speakers and half-clad bodies writhed to the beat, swilling drinks from plastic cups.

When I reached the stage, Jazz smiled down at me with her hands on her hips, looking like Wonder Woman or some such Amazon queen. She hadn't even opened her mouth to sing and she already commanded the stage. She was dressed in all white, contrasting her dark hair and olive skin. I noticed she wore a pair of white snakeskin boots. God, she had nice boots.

I went to the side of the stage and climbed the steps. Lala came over and took my guitar case.

"Nervous?" she asked.

"Perpetually," I replied, looking over the house gear. I made adjustments on the amplifier.

"Sound check in ten," Lala said.

"Guitar stand?" I asked.

She pointed behind the amp and sailed to the other side of the stage. I watched her lovingly remove her bass guitar from its case, polishing the neck with a special cloth. When she shrugged under the strap, I swear I could hear her sigh with pleasure. Lala was a true musician and she wasn't kidding when she said without music she'd die. She was an attractive woman, unique to some people's taste, but with her guitar around her neck she transformed into a true rock goddess. Maybe I should stop being selfish and let her have the songs.

I wasn't a true musician, I just played guitar. Don't get me wrong, I loved to play my guitar but I was a writer first. The songs were my contribution to the band. They were merely poems turned to lyrics framed by music, poems I had written long before I'd met any of them. That was why it was hard to let them go. I hoped Jazz wouldn't forget the words again.

Mags bounded up the steps wearing a pair of red, tightly fitting men's boxer briefs and a yellow sports bra.

"Hey, Squirrely!" Jazz called to her. "You forgot to put on your clothes!"

Mags laughed. "The squirrel is in a better place and you're lucky I'm wearing this much."

"Is he in squirrel heaven?" I ribbed her.

"He might be, but I'm in pussy heaven for sure!" Mags said, surveying the audience. "I'll take one of you, and one of you," she said, pointing to different girls in the crowd. She yanked her drumsticks from the back of her briefs and smacked them together. "Let's roll!"

I strapped on my guitar and attached my remote to my belt. I hadn't been tethered to an amp since Jazz unplugged me once by mistake. It had thrown off my entire performance that night. She knew I didn't like to be touched while I played. Lala didn't mind Jazz grinding all over her, but I did. I tuned my guitar and chuckled in spite of myself. Man, I really was uptight.

Jazz signaled the soundman and the dance music stopped. She stepped to up the microphone and stared into the horde, making eye contact with a pretty girl near the front of the stage. Jazz slid her hand slowly up and down the mic stand. Lala and I grinned at each other from opposite sides of the stage. It was Jazz turning on the audience before she uttered a single note. Jazz gripped the mic in her palms, closed her eyes, and heaved a long, sexy sigh. It sounded like ahhhhhhhhh and then became ohhhhhhhhh and then mmmmmmmm. Then tossed her head back, and simulated an orgasm. The crowd remained silent and breathless. Somewhere in the sea of her captives, someone hollered, "Whooooooo!"

When Jazz finished she smiled and fanned herself with her hand. She looked over at me and asked into the mic, "Is it hot in here or is it just me?"

"No, it's just you," I said, grinning.

"Then you better heat up your side of the stage!" Jazz said.

At her command, I played my usual warm-up riff, slowly working my guitar into a scream that rivaled Jazz's fake orgasm. Mags clicked her sticks above her head, keeping my time.

"Sinclair Stevens, everyone!" Jazz announced as I played.

I was shy and barely looked up from my guitar. I didn't care about the applause, but it was nice that the audience was already engaged.

"Lala! Show them what you've got!" Jazz said.

Lala showed off her infinite skills with a funky pop and slap line from a song called "Take Me Down."

"Don't stop, Lala, keep it going," Jazz said. "LuAnn Abernathy, everyone!" Then Jazz turned to me and gave me a nod to start the rhythm to the song.

"Mags! Let's go, I need the beat! Give it to me, girl!" Jazz yelled.

Mags started to play and the audience went wild. And that was just the sound check.

Jazz called a song and we played it and she was right, it was fun. Our first set was over before I knew it. From the heavy applause and cheers, it was obvious they liked us. It was bittersweet. I hadn't realized how much I'd missed playing with them. I didn't miss our combustive off-stage drama, but our musical chemistry was still red hot.

We took a ten-minute break. Mags and Lala ventured into the crowd, Mags in pursuit of her next ex-lover and Lala, per usual, mingling with her new fans. I unstrapped my guitar and rested it in the guitar stand, then I sat down to decompress on the top step leading off the stage.

A waiter sailed over to me bearing a cocktail and a bottle of water. I graciously accepted the water but declined the drink.

"No, thanks, I don't drink alcohol while I play," I said.

"Okay," he said, shrugging. "I'll tell her you don't want it. But you're dumb because she's really hot and she was thoughtful enough to send a water."

I scanned the crowd and found *her* staring at me with a sweet smile. "Hold on," I called the waiter back. "On second thought, I'll take the drink."

He smirked. "I thought so."

It was a Grey Goose martini with three olives. I raised the glass in thanks. She stared into my eyes and sipped her drink. This time her gaze said she knew me, and I felt the same familiar bond. I got up with the intention of thanking her face to face, when Jazz swooped over and snatched the glass from my hand.

"I'm pretty sure this was meant for me," she said, tossing back the martini in a few gulps. She laughed and stuffed an olive in my mouth. "Stay on the porch, puppy, I saw her first."

I stood there, like a mute idiot as Jazz blazed her way through the crowd and toward the object of my desire. It didn't take long for Jazz to have the woman laughing. They both turned to glance at me, the blonde offering me a look akin to pity. The glint in Jazz's eye cut me like a knife. She didn't even like blondes. And, yes, I was a brunette when Jazz and I first met.

I turned away from them and skulked to the back of the stage. I tuned my guitar and got ready for the next set.

Jazz bounded on stage and found me. "Guess who has a date later?" she taunted.

"You Jazz, you, you, you," I said.

"That's right," she said, flipping her hair. "Me!"

"What did you say to her? I saw how she looked at me."

"Oh, just that you'd gone through a recent break-up and swore a vow of celibacy because you can't ever imagine yourself being with another woman. You are *just* that heart-broken."

"Oh really? Seriously, is that what you think?"

"Well, it has been three years since we broke up and I don't believe you've had a single date."

"How would you know? You haven't been around."

Jazz put her hand on her hip. "Well? Have you?"

"No," I muttered.

"It obviously takes a long time to get over *this*," Jazz said, pointing to herself.

I scowled as she strutted away and watched her grab the microphone. Part of me thought she just might make an announcement to the crowd that I was still hopelessly in love with her. Thankfully, she just hollered, "We're baaaaaack!"

I said, "God, you're a bitch," under my breath.

Jazz glanced back at me as if she heard my comment and gave me a thunderous look. I knew what she was doing. She had no real interest in that woman.

As you may guess, the rest of the night didn't hold the same zeal. I ignored Jazz on stage and played from the shadows.

When we were done, I packed up my guitar and headed back to my room without a word to anyone.

"Sin! Wait!" Mags called after me. "We have to sign autographs."

I ignored her and circled the perimeter of the crowd. Autographs, *please*.

Back in my hotel room, I wasted no time trading my clothes for a bathing suit. Donning a pair of linen pants and a matching cover-up, I grabbed a towel and my camera and headed out for some night photography.

If I could have made it from the third floor, I would have hopped down to the beach from my balcony. Instead, I opted for the stairs. The door opened to the white sand and an incandescent moonlit sky. I draped the towel over my shoulder and put the camera strap around my neck. In the distance, the dance music resumed. I imagined Mags scribbling her signature and probably her phone number on napkins to her prospects, Lala off in a corner chatting on the phone with her wife and Jazz in some erotic huddle with the woman of my dreams.

I laid the towel on the sand, pleased that I was mostly alone on the beach. In the distance, a couple strolled along the shore. The cadence of their strides told me they'd been together for years. They had a nice rhythm. I raised my camera and took a series of shots as they appeared in silhouette in front of the moon.

"Original Sin," a voice said from behind me. "Whatcha doing out here all alone?"

I didn't bother to turn around as Jazz approached. "The question is, what are *you* doing out here alone?"

She sat on the towel beside me, too close for my taste. I wriggled away from her.

"She didn't show up," Jazz said, sighing.

"Well that's good news for your girlfriend, I suppose."

"She not my girlfriend, we are just dating. Nothing serious on my part," Jazz said, studying the moon.

"No serious relationship in three years?" I asked, elbowing her. "I guess it takes a long time to get over *this*." I pointed to myself.

"I've been over *you* and under plenty of people since we broke up," Jazz replied with her typical simper.

I raised my camera and snapped her picture.

"Hey! Not so close!" Jazz said backing away. "Delete that! I'm sure it's awful."

I reviewed the picture, giggling. "You're right, it's hideous."

"Delete it," Jazz demanded, grabbing at my camera.

I swung away from her and tucked the camera under my left arm for safekeeping. "No, I need a picture of you to remind me of how cruel you are."

Jazz leaned across me, trying to snatch the camera. "Give it to me!"

I shoved it beyond her reach and said, "No!" I grabbed her by the shoulders and pushed her down onto the sand. "You're never getting it and maybe, just maybe I'll post it all over social media!" I laughed maniacally.

"You better not!" Jazz warned.

I pinned her wrists above her head. "And who's going to stop me?"

Her eyes softened and she smiled up at me. She bit her lower lip and moved against me, making me realize the placement of my body on hers. If I shifted, even slightly, it would only make things worse. I was on a live mine. I could feel her heat through my filmy pants. I never should have traded my jeans for linen.

She arched her back and moaned in her breathy, irresistible way. "Kiss me, Sinclair. I know you want to. I can feel it."

I stared at her mouth as she spoke, remembering the softness of her lips and the sweetness of her tongue. She had always tasted like peppermint.

I released her wrists and stroked her face with my fingers. She gripped my hips and pressed herself into me, staring into my eyes. I moved with her in perfect sync, surrendering to the sensation between my thighs. As my desire rose, my resentment receded. She pulled me close and sighed in my ear, "I've missed this." She raked her fingers through my hair and pulled me into her kiss.

"I knew it!" Lala squealed, staring down at us. "I sure as shit knew it!"

I rolled off Jazz and leapt to my feet.

Jazz sat up slowly, brushing the sand out of her hair. "Can we help you?" Jazz asked.

"No, but I can help you," Lala said with a grin. "Your lawyer lady friend is here looking for you. She said she came in to surprise you. I guess it's a good thing I found you first. Real nice lady, Jazz. She told me that you two just bought a house together. She even invited us all to the housewarming party."

Jazz got up and wiped her hands on her pants. "Where is she?"

"Lobby lounge, darlin'," Lala drawled.

Jazz glanced at me briefly. "You better delete that picture."

"I will," I said. "I will delete that picture. Consider it erased. It's ancient history."

"Thanks for the memories, ladies," Jazz said, walking away.

I felt Lala's eyes on me as I watched Jazz leave. "It's for the best, Sweetums. Jazzy Jazz hasn't changed. Come on back with me, Sin. Let's have a drink together and talk. It's better you knew before you went and got your heart stomped on."

I resisted the urge to correct her grammar, because it was Lala, after all.

"No, you go," I told her. "I need to be alone."

"You don't to want sign autographs?" Lala asked, chuckling.

"No, I do not want to sign autographs," I said. "But I do want you to have the songs."

"Are you serious? For real?"

"I am serious. I can't let my babies die."

Lala hugged me and shrieked, "I'll keep them alive for ya, sugar. I need to call Nancy! Thank you, Sinclair!"

She gave me another full-body hug and then danced her way back to the resort dialing her cell phone.

When she was gone, I shook off the towel and sat down to review the pictures I'd taken. I stared at the one of Jazz for a while before I deleted it. Sardonic was not how I wanted to remember her. My lips still tingled from her kiss, not to mention other areas. However, I felt the grip on my heart release. I suppose that's what closure feels like. It was liberating, at least.

I scanned the photos until I came to the one of the woman on the beach. Somehow, I saw my future in her eyes. Of course, that notion was ridiculous. Was it possible to fall in love with someone from a picture? I felt a presence behind me and figured it was Mags' turn to coax me back to the party.

"Is it true you aren't signing autographs?"

It wasn't Mags. This voice was sexy with a hint of a Tennessee drawl, southern but different from Lala's heavy Georgia twang.

She sat down beside me and placed a book in my lap. "Could I persuade you to sign this?"

It was one of my novels.

"I finally recognized you from the picture on the back of your book," she said, turning the book over in my hand.

When her bare arm brushed mine, I shivered. Under the moonlight, her topaz eyes sparkled with intellect. I noticed the freckles on her nose. She leaned back on her palms, stretched out her long legs and stared at the moon, perfectly content in my silence it seemed. I studied her profile.

"I'm Cherokee and Irish," she said.

"What an intriguing ethnic combination," I stated, "beautifully unique."

She glanced over at me and grinned. "I love your work, by the way. It revealed you to me, as did the lyrics to your songs. I hope you found the resolution you needed tonight."

"What do you mean?" I asked, suddenly nervous. "What makes you think I needed resolution?"

"I observed the dynamic between you and Jazz," she said. "I was a pawn in her power play. How could I not notice?"

"Perceptive," I said. "Are you a psychotherapist, or just highly observant?"

"I am a psychology professor," she said, peering at me through a wave of silky hair. "My name is Wendy Wyatt. Dr. Wendy Wyatt."

"Yes, Dr. Wyatt, I did get the closure I didn't even know I needed," I said.

"That's wonderful, Sinclair," she said, smiling. She took the book from me and stared at my picture on the back. "Do you think it's possible to fall in love with someone based on a photograph? I'm doing a paper on the theory of love at first sight."

I clutched my camera in my lap and nodded. "Yes, I do."

"Would you care to discuss it over a drink?" She rose and offered me her hand. "I have a pen in my room. You can just sign the book to Wendy."

That is the beginning of another story...

BEALTAINE

Anjuli Sherin

two lovers begin

amidst the green woods

at start of spring

when all life is rising

rising up from the dark

and one spells a knot with the love that she brings

and the other, she knows it not

white flowers they slip silken fingered through their hair

and such is the marvel

the curve of her cheek is one

her hand never forgot

and the light, oh the light

spilled down through the branches

glancing on every precious thing

light golden hair, soft earlobes

pearl white and milky brown skin

light lingered amidst the shadows

where murmured promises were given in voices dim

and such was the marvel

even the stars

woke at that noon hour
and watched from afar

and bore witness, last witness
to love

long after the day did depart.

FOOTNOTES

Erin L. Cork

Stopped at a red light, Malfunction Junction. A seventies model Chevy pickup ahead of me, bull balls dangle from the trailer hitch and a faded bumper sticker that was probably added when the truck was new, "Disco Sucks." There's a man-child anywhere between the ages of 18 and 30 in the driver's seat. It could be a hand-me-down, his father's rig.

I'll never share the memory of peeling the backside from that sentiment and slapping it on the tailgate in front of me. But I do have a scrapbook full of goose-bump gospel moments in the fellowship of outcasts.

"The anti-disco slogan, 'Disco Sucks' available on t-shirts, bumper stickers, buttons and more…" Luis-Manuel Garcia explains, *"…wasn't just a metaphor in the '70s: it was a direct reference to cock-sucking, aiming a half-spoken homophobic slur at disco and its fans."*

I came of age in queer bars. I'm not gonna lie, I had some moves. I'm like Pavlov's dog when I hear the thump of a drum machine and the pulse of a synthesizer. My shoulders roll, hips gyrate, feet slide and arms rise towards swirling colors real or imagined.

The light turns green, a new generation on my playlist; Janelle Monáe's "Django Jane" revs into the speaker, volume up, foot on the pedal I'm singing along, head nodding. I'm as fired up as ever.

My education began in earnest in the basement of the Palace Hotel and house parties in the late seventies. I was still in my teens. I was reading *Our Bodies, Ourselves*, Rita Mae Brown and Patricia Nell Warren. Holy Shit, I wasn't alone.

* * *

House parties grew into clubs. We danced to meet each other, to be together, to celebrate. We were outcasts in high schools and hometowns. We were weirdos filled with shame but when we twirled and moved, sang out "Don't Leave Me This Way", "I Will Survive" and "We Are Family," always ending our nights with "Last Dance," it was with a fist in the air.

It was life schooling. I enrolled in advanced courses of acceptance and denial, hitting the floor with an earnestness I had previously reserved for class officer campaigns; "*Voulez vous coucher avec moi ce soir, Voulez vous coucher avec moi*"?

In 1979 radio D.J Steve Dahl lit the fuse on the Disco Sucks movement in Chicago where he blew up disco records in Comiskey Park at a baseball game. AIDS was new and on the rise, terrifying the club scene. Confusion about what it was and how you might catch it contributed to the backlash.

Fran Lebowitz commented on the events, "*There's music I don't like, but I don't make a career out of not liking it-I just don't listen to it. 'Disco Sucks' was kind of a panic on the part of straight white guys. Disco was basically black music, rock 'n' roll was basically white: those guys felt displaced.*" A familiar refrain today, a scratchy record on repeat.

About the same time the assault on Disco was picking up speed my parents split for good. My father left his longtime teaching job in a local

64

high school after falling in love with his student teacher, a young man in his mid-twenties, closer to my age than my dad's. Pop came out in a blaze of glory or burning bridges depending on which angle you looked at it. He moved to Portland and went to work for the "Oregonian."

Thinking about it now, I may have wanted him to hang his own balls from his rearview mirror like he had dice in his Northern Montana College days. I guess this might really be a sign of castration. These are steers, not bulls. Whatever. Anyway, I wanted him to be my dad again, not the poster child for a mid-life crisis. I jumped in my '66 Dodge Pickup, a retired forest service truck that I had painted sky blue, and followed him out west.

I pulled into the city, both cocky and overwhelmed as I went the other way on a one-way. I had a meager savings, a typewriter and big dreams, muted and muddled but recurring. Dad and I had some reparation to be done. At least I thought so. His part included subsidizing my writing ambition. After all, he had created and nurtured this monster. He couldn't just walk away.

But the transformation he was going through had nothing to do with fatherhood. He was trying to leave his past, all of it behind. I wasn't going to make it easy for him. After all, this was about me.

In the beginning of this contract I wrote by day. I was working on a brilliant debut novel about a talking dog that had witnessed the murder of his mistress, stunning the world when he exposed the killer that had tried to silence him with peanut butter. Ha, who wouldn't want to read this?

At night, Dad and I would hit the town. A weird and tentative twist on our relationship. I wasn't old enough to drink but I had swagger. In my black polyester pants, matching vest, white t-shirt and cowboy hat that may have had a feather in it, I must have been hard to resist. We'd dance until the bars closed then work all day. Eventually, the arrangement got uncomfortable. Watching my father cruise was unsettling. I started venturing out to different clubs on my own like The Other Side of Midnight, Embers and Aaron's.

* * *

I was shaking my stuff to "A Taste of Honey" with a local DJ who had befriended me when a small, beautiful dark-haired woman moved in and up on me. She winked at the other woman, pulled me away and into her.

This was Kris, a local attorney in her thirties. She fed me maraschino cherries from her amaretto sours. I'd practice tying the stems in a knot with my tongue.

Kris treated me well, took me to concerts, the theatre and barbecues with her friends. She'd pack a picnic lunch, her secret recipe potato salad. We'd drive into the mountains in my pickup that she claimed was a chick magnet. We'd lie on a blanket by a stream where I continued my lessons. We'd laugh hard and loud. I'd tell her about all the stories I wanted to write. She'd kiss me and tell me that she believed I could do anything. At night, we'd go dancing. God, I loved to dance.

Dad wanted me to find work if I was going to stay. Supporting the night life for both of us was taking a financial toll. I tried to convince him that I was working. My novel was my job, he was a patron of the arts. Unconvinced, he wanted me to contribute to the household, pay rent and help with the utilities. In a fit of rage and abandonment issues I left. I drove back to Montana where I found refuge in the arms and house of my high school sweetheart. I went to school and found a part time job.

Disco wasn't dying, it was alive and well. I sought out house parties with the music cranked where I could find my groove again. I needed the fix. I felt alive on the dance floor with a girl running her hands over my body and whispering in my ear.

* * *

Later we'd have makeshift clubs of our own like the AMVETS and Daddy's. These were our safe havens away from the slurs, mumbled hostilities, nasty shout-outs and bashings. We found refuge under the rainbow tent, in our big ol' queer revivals.

I struggled to settle down, met another girl who would eventually get me to Seattle where I would let the colored lights and thumping beats take hold again.

I just wanted to dance. When we split in the mid-eighties I gravitated toward the clubs like Neighbours where I would spend my weekends shouting and singing, going home with miss "right now."

Our community though was experiencing devastating losses, our brightest, most creative men, our friends were sick. They were dying.

I have a painting that hangs on my wall done by Seattle artist Matthew Luzny. I shared a house with Matt. He had a quick, dry wit and a bark of a laugh. He'd whip his shirt from his lean and muscled body.

He'd shake, shake, shake in the heat of release. He loved light and color. Oh the things he could do with texture, glass and paint. He had vision.

I'd met him through an artist I was dating. His diagnosis was perplexing and stunning. We didn't know what to make of it. He and I had talked about having a kid together. The reality of such a venture was just the beginning of what we would come to understand about HIV and AIDS.

The "we" was taken out of it because I would never fully comprehend what it meant to live with the disease, the terror of a sore throat progressing to a full-blown cold. Matt died in 1994 at the age of 36.

In her book, *Hot Stuff: Disco and the Remaking of American Culture*, Alice Echols says, "*Lesbianism has never carried the same cachet as male homosexuality in either the music business or in disco studies. Disco's only self-declared and unambiguously lesbian performer, Alicia Bridges, came out twenty years after she scaled the charts with her 1978 hit "I Love the Nightlife" And yet lesbian and bisexual women were part of disco culture-both in their own bars and in gay male and mixed clubs.*"

Our history like history in general centers on men even in gay history. The dances and parties were filled with women too. These men were our brothers, we danced and sweated right along with them but little of it is documented. We participated in the seduction, the lure, our own sexual awakenings side by side.

- In the first minutes of January 1st, 2014, Musab Mohamed Masmari dumped gasoline down a stairwell at Neighbours the popular Seattle gay club. The 750 people inside escaped without injury, certainly not the attacker's intent.

- On June 24th, 1973, an arsonist set fire to the Upstairs Lounge in New Orleans.

- On February 21, 1997, the American terrorist Eric Rudolph set off an explosion at the Otherside Lounge in Atlanta.

- October 6, 1998, Matthew Shepard was beaten and left for dead near Laramie, Wyoming.

- September 22, 2000, Ronald Gay opened fire in a gay bar in Roanoke, VA, killing one and injuring another six.

- On March 1st, 2009, Lawrence and Lawrneil Lewis along with their cousin Alejandro Gray launched chunks of concrete at customers in a gay bar in Galveston, TX.

- On June 12, 2016, Omar Mateen shot and killed 49 people and wounded 53 others in Orlando's Pulse nightclub.

- June 28th, 1969, a police raid at the Stonewall Inn in New York caused an uprising and led to gay pride marches. Pride as we know it.

We cut loose. We were free. We got to be with people who understood. When you say, "Disco Sucks", you can't comprehend how we found one another or the way our bodies moved together. The risk involved was everything. It's how we created community.

I love Disco. Dance music. It's not the only music I love, I'll put my eclectic collection up against anyone's but I won't be embarrassed by the 12" mixes that have contributed to my education as much as any lecture I sat through. Stonewall, discos, the seventies helped us find and shape our identities. It didn't suck.

"I'm Coming Out" is an anthem we scream and shout. Don't stop the dance.

SMEAR THE QUEER

John Jeffire

—for Kristine and Lea

Our smaller selves found no shortage
Of ways to shame the sensibilities of
The men some would one day become.
Listen and you still hear the cracking
Voice of puberty call out to the pack
Of mismatched socks and torn jackets
And kneeless jeans, behold the wave of
Churning legs bursting toward the far
Playground fence to safety, those in
The middle intent on corralling victims
To the ground. Remember when old
Whitey drove Harvey to the dirt?
Run all he wanted, but wasn't nobody
Going to the Principal over that
Flat out creaming. And the time
Matty was rammed against the fence
And ganged by Rusty and Aaron?
Damn, smeared his nose all across
His girly face. And who didn't laugh
When Plato got drilled by Straight Hair
Willie and we high-fived to heaven?

At the teacher's whistle, we buried ourselves

In our smallnesses, years later to be outed

In public charades and masques of shame—

On those phobic fields of churned turf,

We learned to perpetrate the rabid little

Lynchings we as soon learned to forget,

Oblivious to those condemned and hunted

In blind boyhood's hangman complicity.

ON JUDY GARLAND

Brian Kirst

As a gay man and a self-described film buff, I've had a love-hate relationship—with a stronger emphasis on the negative side of the highway—with Judy Garland for years now.

It didn't start out that way. As a kid, I totally adored her. In fact, being a very theatrical kindergartener, I even decided that one day we'd marry and do countless summer stock productions and films together. If I recall correctly, I announced this, with gusto and determination, at a family dinner one Sunday. The shock I felt upon being told of her death had me reeling, from room to room, asking various relatives, over and over again, if this life-altering news was really true. Sadly, they all confirmed it was.

As a teen, though, I eventually discovered the grittier charms of artists like Marianne Faithfull and Nico and Ronnie Spector—whose lifestyles, coincidentally, echoed some of the more addictive excesses of Garland's—and soon began to find her go-for-broke performing style a bit too forceful and bombastic for the ever-expanding subtlety in my tastes. The late-night movies I adored also faded in importance next to the thrills of gory horror films on cable and the (seemingly) heterosexual charms of the smooth studs on my mother's soap operas.

Honestly, discovering that Garland was a gay icon, didn't sit well with me either. There is no self-hate like the self-hate of a gay man and I was determined not to fall into the trap of being some skinny, stereotypical lover of the traditional female diva. As I grew older, I did, begrudgingly, begin to appreciate the seasoned Garland's subdued take on poignant Noel Coward numbers and the like, but I have never been able to regain my early fascination and devout appreciation for her as a performer. But it turns out, she has never been far from my interests—even though I would have adamantly sworn otherwise.

As someone who writes about horror as a hobby, I am often asked, whether it be on panel discussions or in friendly conversations with other devotees, where my love for the genre began. Looking back, I can definitely remember discovering my favorite *Friday the 13th* film—*Part 3*, for those keeping score. It ran nonstop, one summer on HBO, and confirmed my interest in the genre would be lifelong and not just some passing fancy. As with many others, John Carpenter's *Halloween* definitely raised my pre-teen hackles, as well. But if I truly and honestly trace it back, my love for horror actually began with Garland. For many, her iconic portrayal of Dorothy in *The Wizard of Oz* meant a world of hopeful fantasy and countless concert renditions of "Over the Rainbow" —a song I simply cannot stand, by the way. But one Sunday evening, she introduced the four-year-old me to a world of evil witches and terrifying flying monkeys. She transported me to an environment far beyond the commonplace dangers I witnessed in my small town— brawling factory workers, drunken farmers, angry parents—and gave me something far more exotic. I knew the characters that she faced as Dorothy Gale were scary, but they were colorful and…imaginary. And…they were survivable.

Thus, Garland opened me up to the worlds that I would eventually discover on the fragile cusp of manhood. This bountiful gesture is still paying off to this day. Every time I discover some rare slasher on a dusty

VHS tape in a thrift store and meet another previously hereto unknown terror actress to adore, I have her to thank. When I bond in restaurants with strangers over our various obscure horror film t-shirts, she is at the heart of it. When I gather with sleep-worn friends for B-Movie Marathons and we become family because of it, her essence is somewhere in that room.

Many years ago, her death arguably inspired a group of courageous drag queens to stand up for the rights of the LGBT community in an incredibly inspiring and visible way. But, her life—at least her performing life—inspired me to my own rebellion. Every time my father grumbled over me reading another horror novel or purchasing the latest issue of "Fangoria," I was standing my ground, for the first time, for something I loved. Something that was sparked in me by watching her perky, pigtail-sporting adventuress, all those years ago, and, from this moment on, I will never downplay the significance of that starting point.

So, viva, la Garland! May you rest in peace upon every laurel that is, deservedly, thrown your way!

AT THE RED LIGHT, A MEMORY

Ben Kline

about that short, blonde CrossFitter

who had that three-haired skin tag

dangling from his throat

like a dried crow,

who left me

cropped me out of photos

my friends could yet click,

who introduced me to

his new college-ruled husband

at the Arts & Sciences mixer,

congratulating me on making tenure,

mistaking my side hug and smile

for warm regards, sliding

his damp fingertip

across my taut sacrum,

scooping slightly into my hairy cleft

like a small, piloted drone searching
for paper or cotton, maybe wood

or even lace chrysanthemums
for his queen, but I

had only brick fists
and a succinct list of forgiven not forgotten

tattooed in raven's blood
along my right cephalic vein

pulsing like every neutron
impatient for the end,

for the punch
served next and quickly downed.

CHANGING I'S

Jarred Thompson

It occurred to me on a Tuesday morning that Trevor had a thing for Janice. It was the way he'd always laugh at her rude jokes, begging her for more to make the morning march toward midday bearable. Being out in the sun and laying bricks all day wasn't an easy job. It required a mindless commitment to the dumb hardness of hot stone that grew hotter as the day edged closer to twilight.

"So I said to the lady...*jirre* bitch can you put some underarm on sometime, fuck, you smell like old *vetkoek* oil and rotten sardines." Janice waved the flag ushering traffic around the construction site. Her stories always lightened the morning mood of the others and they accepted me only because we were close friends.

"Must we really work with a *moffie*?" Craig, the team leader, said when I first started working with the guys. I knew brick laying wasn't the ideal job for me but money was hard to come by at home and I needed a quick job to help Ma with the rent. That's where Janice came in.

"Just come work with us man. The work is hard and the pay is *kak* but hey it's something for the time being."

"Fine Janice. But it won't be for long. I don't wanna be one of those scum that fry their brains in the sun all day laying stupid bricks for other people to walk on."

She gave me this disappointed look; she'd been working there for 3 years now and had had trouble finding another job. I felt bad for what I said, but I didn't tell her. Janice was beautiful, she knew that, and so did a lot of guys. But I think she enjoyed getting dirty and dusty with the guys at work. She enjoyed covering her beauty in the manual labor that dried out her skin and caked dust all over her body. It was as if she was secretly defiling her God-given beauty, and taking pleasure in doing so too.

"Hey Janice, you want some of my chicken mayo?" Trev unlatched his red lunchbox revealing two toasted sandwiches.

"Yeah, sure honey." I watched Janice sit down next to Trev, her sweat trailing down her long neck and disappearing into the narrow valley between her breasts. Janice and I always had our lunches together and naturally I sat down next to her. Trev shot a rancid look in my direction but I chose to ignore it, placing all my attention on my peanut butter sandwiches.

Janice and Trev were locked in conversation, a conversation meant to exclude me, while I struggled to work the peanut butter in my mouth into manageable pieces to swallow. The day was sweltering with layers of heat rising from the tar road, being packed tighter and thicker in the atmosphere. The longer we worked, the hotter it got, the wider the circles of sweat on our yellow work overalls became. Heat, in any form, always brought what lurked underneath to the surface. Be it sweat, body odor, or the sulphuric smells of David, a fellow worker whose fart had the potency of chloroform.

"You should come out with the boys to Uncle Greg's later for a drink and a splif." Trev mumbled through his half-eaten sandwich.

"Oh can my lovie here come with?" Janice rested her head on my shoulder and I caught a draft of her saltiness, a sea-like smell that was deathly sweet in my nostrils. I wasn't attracted to Janice as much as I

80

longed to be her. To be looked at the way guys looked at her. To have random men whistle at me, lick their lips and click their fingers in my direction. It was a desire I never spoke about, but felt in the rigidness of my hips. Trev looked at me then, his hazel eyes catching the sun in a violent way. I had to look away for fear that I'd stare too long and give away some part of myself in the process.

"Sure…the moffie can join."

"Shut up don't call him that!" She pinched his arm with her long purple nails. The nails I helped her paint the night before.

"Eina, fuck Janice, your nails are like claws!" Trev jerked up and rubbed his arm, looking if she left a mark. Janice laughed and made a cat-like hiss at him arching her fingers into a claw.

"So I guess I will see both of you later then?" said Trev, moving to pack away his things and get back to work.

"Yes you will." I blurted out. Janice looked at me, her eyebrows raised and her head tilted to one side. I swallowed hard on the peanut butter still left clinging to the inside of my cheeks.

That night we all met at Uncle Greg's around 7:30. It was a hole-in-the-wall kind of place with crates used for stools and posters of bikini-clad women plastered on the walls. The smoke of cigarettes and weed made everyone appear blurred and out of focus.

"What will you two be having then?" Uncle Greg, a wrinkled man with a crooked nose asked us as he wiped the inside of a glass.

"Two beers uncle." I said, holding up two fingers and shouting over the base from the speakers that pounded our eardrums. The rest of the crew were here already, most of them drunk. We soon left the bar and joined the others.

"So you two finally decided to drink with the rest of us?" David belched, making Janice and I side-eye each other. He moved to one side of the bench making space for the two of us. My eyes inevitably found Trev's face, settling on observing the subtle movements of him transferring his drink to the cusp of his pink lips. He looked different outside of the yellow overalls, as if he'd shed a second skin. He wore blue jeans with a buttoned-up black shirt that seemed too formal for a place like this. His hair was combed back and his face appeared brighter.

Janice and I sat down with her soon becoming the center of attention among the guys. She began relaying a story I had heard quite often from her: the time she peed in her boyfriend's car after she caught him in bed with one of her girlfriends.

"So there I was right, staring through the window at those *naaiers*. And I was perfectly calm, so calm that I actually scared myself. Well then you know what I did? I went inside, took their car keys from the kitchen counter and went to go pee in the back seat of both of their cars."

The group fell apart into laughter, some slapping their knees, others guffawing. I wondered if they would find Janice as funny if she wasn't as breathtakingly beautiful. But Trev wasn't laughing as much as the others. Instead, he smiled and shifted his body lightly from side to side, all the while watching Janice intently.

The night continued much like that, with Janice telling one of her crazy stories about men and the group listening, hungry for each honeyed word that dripped from her delicate mouth. We drank and smoked more, the night becoming darker, while Uncle Greg's started taking on the dimension of a sauna. Glistening sweat had formed on all our brows and the alcohol seemed to make us sweat even more.

"Uncle Greg, open a door or put on a fan or something man. It's *kak* hot in here." Trev shouted, already solidly intoxicated and slurring his words a little. Soon a few windows were opened and the chilled evening air made us all breathe lighter. We all pushed the crates and benches to one side and started dancing.

Music filled the limbs of everyone with a vigor that was electric and consuming. Feet tapped the ground, bodies swerved round, back and forth, others whistled and jeered as the beats of the night transformed from one song into another. It was the first time I felt like one of the others, a working man out with his buddies shedding off the weight of the numbing daily grind. Eventually people started pairing off, guy with girl, girl with guy, until I was left with Nicole. She was the type of girl that always had a blank look on her face, as if she lived a serene life, yet everyone knew that Nicole had just come out of prison on account of assaulting another woman who'd looked at her man a bit too enthusiastically. We weren't very close, Nicole and I, but she smiled at me in a demur way and outstretched her arms toward me on the dance floor as if she were preparing to coddle a baby. I looked around to see where Janice had gone, but through the crowd of stomping feet and hip-thrusting I couldn't spot her.

"I'm just going to the bathroom quick." I mouthed to Nicole over the loud music, attempting to make my way through the crowd of people that packed Uncle Greg's to capacity. The room had gotten hotter now, the chilled night air not enough to quell this mass of human heat burning in ecstatic release.

I turned the corner and headed outside to where the toilets stood: four pillars of plastic in the moonlight. The night was quiet, except for a few dogs barking, as I staggered to one of the toilets. My head felt off-balance like something heavy had been put on one side of its scale. I closed my eyes as I let out my pee, sighing sweetly and slowly feeling my body come back to its senses. It was then that I heard a rocking, a strange clapping sound that sounded like flesh on flesh. The rocking grew more violent and I decided to follow the sound to its source.

Behind one of the out houses was a tree whose branches twisted over the yard, hanging heavy with the tiny bulbs of mulberries. It was against this tree that I saw Trev up against Janice, his hands down her pants and her hands clawing into his back. Her mouth was open as if she wanted to say something but her face tightened with each thrust of Trev's hand. There seemed to be two forces rising from her body, one of protest and acquiescence.

I hid in the shadow of one of the cars parked in the yard and watched them move against and with each other, their mouths pressed onto each other's skin in a kind of desperation. In a quick movement, Trev spun Janice around and pulled down his blue jeans. I wanted to look away, I wanted to go back inside and resume my dance with Nicole, but he was majestic in the moonlight. His clenching buttocks like a beating heart, the muscles of his legs standing like tree trunks, silent and cool.

I had become so engrossed in watching them that I didn't realize I had moved into full view of the two of them. Trev moved Janice's hair to one side with the brush of his hand and when he did his eye caught my shadow in the distance. Janice was entranced in a hypnotic rhythm with her face looking the other way, but Trev saw me.

His facial expression didn't change; his bodily movements didn't jerk in embarrassment. Instead, he kept his eyes on me even as he kissed Janice's neck and nibbled on her earlobe. His eyes, dark orbs containing sparks of moonlight, seemed to suspend me indefinitely inside of them.

He wanted me there.

I felt my desire exposed like a raw nerve and he seemed to relish in it. I wanted to go back inside, to forget the whole thing, but his gaze transfixed me. An unspoken barrier dissolved between us and for a brief moment I didn't feel like myself. I felt unnaturally pure, free of everything but the moon, the mulberry tree and the two bodies rocking against its trunk.

He broke eye contact with me when he orgasmed, thrusting in quick short bursts against Janice whose hair whipped up and back against his face, covering it from view. I snuck back inside after that, ordering a drink before the bar closed and sitting down to gather my thoughts.

"Where'd you go for so long? I was waiting for you." Nicole came up and sat down beside me. I didn't answer her, still holding the drink to my lips and letting the liquid ebb over the precipice of my mouth.

"You're okay sweetheart?" Janice said, coming to sit beside me.

"Your friend doesn't look too good," said Nicole, holding her hand to my forehead.

"I think it's time to go. You've had enough." Janice took the glass out of my hand and placed it on the floor.

"Yeah we should go." I eventually replied, getting up and looking around the room for Trev. He was by the bar talking, drinking and laughing with Uncle Greg. He chugged a glass of golden liquid down his throat and I watched his Adam's Apple pulse in titillation to the alcohol absolving his taste buds which no doubt still contained traces of Janice.

The next day I watched the two of them the way a detective would watch a suspect in an interrogation room. I looked for subtle signs that they were thinking of the night before: a raised head to the blazing sun, a slow thoughtful wipe of a brow, or a wink in the direction of each other. But there was nothing. In fact, Janice and Trev worked separately all day and didn't so much as exchange a friendly glance.

I kept the image of the two of them against the mulberry tree in my mind. I tried to imagine the two of them from different angles, how the moonlight would have looked against their bodies from a bird's-eye view, how their lust would have smelt mingled with the decayed fruitiness of the mulberries if I was close enough to smell them. Such thoughts kept the immediacy of the heat away, and diverted my attention from the throbbing hangover that whipped at my temples.

"What's for lunch today lovie?" Janice sat down next to me, taking out a cigarette and lighting it. With her first pull of the cigarette her body softened and she unbuttoned her yellow overall slightly, allowing the smell of her strawberry perfume to swell the air around us.

"Same thing as always, peanut butter. I thought you were quitting?"

"I am…it's just I need this, just for today. This hangover is working on my *poes*." She drew phlegm from the back of her mouth and spat it out into the dust road in front of us.

"*Sies* Janice, that's disgusting man."

"Ag relax it's just spit. I'm sure you've seen worse things."

"What does that mean?" I turned to look at her but instead caught Trev's eye in the distance. He was eating chips with David on the other corner, his fingers red with tomato sauce. I couldn't make out clearly which one of us he was watching but he was definitely looking in our direction. I had never yearned for someone else's thoughts as much as I did then.

"You know you gays. You guys are something else."

"I'm not like that Janice. You know that."

"I know…I know…you're saved and all of that. Well done."

I hated talking religion with Janice. She never believed there was any real purpose to our lives. She'd told me that many times when I'd have to hold her hair back over a stranger's toilet bowl every time she got a little too drunk.

"The only thing that matters, lovie, is the will to survive. Turn yourself into the bigger predator in this urban jungle. It's cut-throat out there, and if you're not going to be cut-throat too then…well…expect to bleed."

I remembered her words so vividly, it was the one time I believed I saw through the thorniness of her character. I wanted to believe that something else directed our lives; I wanted to feel that there were forces outside of our control because if there were then maybe my life didn't depend entirely on me.

A week later we were back at Uncle Greg's: the music blaring, the cool night air trying desperately to weave itself in between the cramped sweating bodies of dancers, drinkers, and people who sat and watched each other all night. I had followed a group of guys out back to smoke some *zol*, good strong stuff that came from Durban.

"Fuck man Craig is such a bullshitter. He was supposed to have paid us a week ago gents." Marco blew out a puff of smoke, the soothing smell of marijuana whetting my taste buds for a drag.

"I agree. We should complain." I said, drawing the group's attention to me. They had begun to grow accustomed to my presence around them, yet there were moments, like this one, where I felt like I was put on display. Sort of like a spectacle that they were interested in watching.

"See even *this* guy agrees." David snorted, making the others giggle a little. I ignored the giggling and waited for my turn to smoke.

I lingered behind after the rest of the guys went inside, deciding to enjoy my high away from the crowd of interlocked bodies crisscrossing each other on the dancefloor. I staggered to the pavement and sat down outside Uncle Greg's yard. There was something about how *zol* opened you up to the world, as if your skin became the skin of water and your thoughts were skipping stones across an endless lake. I turned to look down the street and spotted Trev standing by his car shouting on the phone to someone.

"Come on baby it's not like that! Why you gotta bring up money now huh? I told you I'll give you money for the child's school fees. As soon as my money comes in! Fuck why you so impatient?"

He kicked the wheel of his car and put the phone down, drawing out a cigarette to smoke. I suddenly grew nervous realizing that he'd have to pass me to get into Uncle's Greg yard again. Yet as afraid of him as I was I didn't move, the *zol* offering an excuse to stay put and ride out the situation.

I listened to his footsteps growing louder, the subtle clink of the chain around his neck indicating his closeness. I felt his shadow cut across my body as I stared up into the orange streetlight in front of me and as soon as the moment came it ended. I got up, my eyes playing tricks with the orange streetlight deliberately bringing it into and out of focus, when a body—muscular and firm—flung me against the hood of a black car close by. The heat of the engine lingered against my cheek and the smell of tobacco surrounded me.

"You like to watch me?" a breathy voice curled into my ear.

"What?"

"I know you do."

"Leave me alone Trev. What the fuck?"

"Sssshhhh." His hands moved up my legs, crab-like, as if weighing me up for a slaughter. "I'll let you watch…you wanna watch?"

Trev sounded different, as if possessed by an external entity he couldn't understand. It was the closest I'd ever been to him, smelling his mustiness, feeling his rough stubble against my cheek, his body warm and tight around me.

"Yes." Was all I said, closing my eyes as his hands pinched the fat around my stomach.

He let me go after that, disappearing into Uncle Greg's yard and leaving me bent over the hood of the car. I was coming down from my high. The world was restoring its hard dimensions against my senses.

It went on for a couple of weeks. I'd make sure I would be at Uncle Greg's regularly just to catch a glimpse of Trev. Sometimes he'd be there: his hair combed back, his pink lips never too far away from the brim of a glass or bottle. Some nights he wouldn't greet me, wouldn't even acknowledge my existence. And other nights he would be charming a random girl and at the last minute, before they left the bar, he'd glance at me. It was the type of look you'd give to a fellow conspirator, efficient yet filled with meaning. He wanted me to follow them. Sometimes he'd press the girls up against the mulberry tree or against a brick wall of an alley. Other times he'd do it in his car or he'd be conscientious enough to actually take the girl home. These occasions were rare though, since I knew he stayed with his baby mama. On those nights where he'd have the girls moaning in between his sheets I would hop over the low wall and wait below his bedroom window sill. Most nights he'd leave the window slightly ajar for me. In my mind I believed he did that so I could hear the sounds of flesh on flesh, the smells of perfume mutate into earthy sweat and transform into clammy euphoria. For most of these encounters he'd side-eye me with those dark depthless eyes of his. When he orgasmed (usually without bringing his female partner to her climax) he'd look away from me and close his eyes tightly as if saving some intangible part of himself from being seen. I continued in this routine without questions or hesitations because I felt that he had given me a kind of gift that I hadn't fully understood as yet.

NO MONEY NO WORK!

This was the slogan we chanted a month later when Craig informed the workers that the construction company who had hired us was going

90

through some "financial restructuring." As a result, our wages would be delayed for a few weeks . A group of us gathered on a Wednesday morning at the construction site to demand the wages that were due to us.

"These fuckers better pay us. I'm gonna go to Carte Blanche for this bullshit." Janice said, filing her purple nails as she watched the group of workers grow larger and more vocal. It seemed someone had called in their uncles and cousins to join the protest and now people were burning tires in the street and pelting cars with bricks.

"I can't blame them for acting like this. This is bullshit. We need our money. What kind of world do they think we live in?" I said.

"You're finally coming around to my way of thinking huh?" Janice smiled.

"Shut up Janice. I'm just saying. This isn't right at all."

Craig was standing with the managers from headquarters a few blocks away, watching the spectacle unfold. A couple of police vans had arrived already and were watching the commotion unfold with their hands wrapped tightly round their weapons.

Trev was at the forefront of the protest. He had wrapped his yellow overalls to a long stick and had lit it on fire. He was bare-chested, waving round a ball of fire and sending blankets of smoke into the air. I shouted slogans of protest while watching him wave his fiery baton round in the air. There was something primordial about the sight of him wielding fire with his bare skin inches away from the flame.

"Hey Craig you *poes*. We want our money *sonnie*!" Trev yelled. In his anger he appeared almost translucent, imbibed with an energy that infected the crowd which yelled, danced and protested alongside him. It didn't take long after that for rubber bullets to travel through the air and into the crowd. We dispersed like cockroaches, each of us scurrying into the crevices and labyrinthine alleyways of Westbury. I had darted instinctively down the first alleyway I saw and lost sight of Janice in the process. I kept running, making sure that I placed as much distance as possible between myself and the construction site. I couldn't afford to be picked up by the police and put in a holding cell. Ma was home sick and there was no one else to bring in money for rent.

I turned a corner, calculating that I was four blocks away from home. I spotted Trev, sitting on his haunches against a wall overrun with graffiti. He has his head in his hands, his straight black hair falling between his fingers. I noticed he was breathing heavy, his body inflating in violent spasms.

"You okay?" I said.

"Yeah, I'm good. Just adrenaline you know."

"Hectic shit hey?" I smiled at him but he didn't smile back. Instead he looked at me as if I was a stranger.

"You should get going."

"What about you?"

"I'm pretty sure that bitch Craig already signaled me out."

"You can come hide out at my house. Till things cool down."

He raised his hand to shield his eyes from the encroaching sun. I was immobile before him, pushing aside all fears that tugged on my intestines, making me nauseous. He lifted himself off the floor and for a moment he was about to speak when a rapid succession of footsteps came up behind me.

"Hey bra, what you doing here? We gotta get out of here. The *gatas* are right behind us." A guy whose name I never knew but who worked with us pushed past me and nudged Trev in the shoulder. Trev looked at me in a weak, blank way and it was then that I understood who he was and who I was to him.

"Come we go hide out there by Alvin. They won't find us there." Trev responded, nudging the stranger to run ahead of him down the alley. He pressed his lips together, nodded in my direction and ran after his friend. I was left there standing in front of a wall of graffiti which featured the eerie image of a man ripping a chunk of flesh from his chest and grinning wildly.

The police caught up to Trev eventually. He was charged with destruction of public property and vandalism. The company we all worked for went bankrupt and their assets were liquidated. It didn't take long for the local municipality to pick up the slack and employ us under a new company who'd just won the construction tender. I didn't go back to work on the site though. There was something about the job that made me think incessantly about Trev: his body in the moonlight under the mulberry tree, his thick limbs all over a subtle meek female body. I found a job at a local library, the quiet smell of books my welcomed solitude to the fast-paced life of Joburg. Ma was recovering from her sickness and I was bringing in enough money to just about cover the rent.

I still saw Janice regularly, usually on the weekends. She had found herself a new man to occupy her time. His name was Delano, a tattooed muscle-bound Malay guy from Cape Town whose favorite pastime was snorting lines of crack. It was strange to watch Janice transform in front of me. Week by week she started losing weight, her skin clinging in desperation to her bones, her hair turning coarse and an odd twitch setting into her movements. She still worked as a laborer but every weekend she'd complain about the heat, dust and the lack of respect she received from the guys at work. Their love for her seemed to sour over time as if her aging beauty was not enough to sustain the magnetic allure she previously held over everyone.

When Trev eventually got out of prison I spotted him near the Somalian grocer one day, washing a Citi Golf with intense fascination. I was on my way to the library at the time, unsure of whether I should stop and greet him. I decided to walk past him, pretending not to know who he was.

"Hey…Joshua right?" He said as I walked past the Golf now fully lathered up in soap.

"Yeah that's right."

"How you been man?"

"I'm…I'm doing good and you Trev?"

"Yeah just fine…getting by."

He had a scar now that ran up the left side of his face and past his eye. I suddenly realized that he was blind in his left eye. There was a pervasive silence between us until he eventually spoke.

"Yeah prison was rough as you can imagine. But you gotta survive you know."

"Well it's good to see you again. Take care of yourself." I wanted to end this awkward conversation. To keep the Trev I knew from the past still alive in my fantasies.

"Wait…We should have a drink sometime." He had that weak blank look in his face again and I remembered the dark sparkling moonlight in his eyes that night I saw him and Janice under the mulberry tree.

"Yeah…maybe." Standing there I became suddenly aware of a deep disappointment that permeated the air around us. In his haggard face I could see the wall of graffiti that he stood in front of all those months ago.

I had no idea who he thought I was or what he expected from me. Too much time seemed to have solidified like a thick layer of lard between us. It occurred to me then—as I submersed myself in the quiet solitude of the library moments later—that nothing and no one was immune from change and maybe, in the end, that was a destructive and liberating thing.

Glossary

vetkoek: a fatty pastry

moffie: derogatory term for a homosexual

kak: shit

naaiers: fuckers

poes: vagina

zol: weed

gatas: slang for police

FREDDIE AT THE BAR

Nicole Pergue

Freddie Mercury's at the bar,
sitting at the corner seat next to me
on a broken down leather stool.
I don't know what he's got
but it's cranberry bright in the glass,
solid pink and salty.

He sips through the thin red straw,
mustache furrowing, lips pursing.
His tight white tee sticks to his chest
and his collar bones rise with breath
as he speaks to me.

    What are you doing here?

I needed to clarify something for myself, I say.

He laughs—
    well, at least look like
    you're having fun—you gotta look like
    you belong here—

he signals for the bartender

to get me a drink,

and he already knows what I want—

a sweet beer, a slice of lemon

wedged in the spout.

I swallow a sour seed

and watch girls,

one after the other,

enter the bar, letting the early

summer light follow behind them.

The flags hanging outside

flutter in and out the door

like wanting hands.

    How does it taste?

Like a temple, I say.

    What are you doing here?

Staring at the liquor mosaic reflecting

backs of glass bottles and

my face, I part my lips—I'm lonely, I say.

Freddie pulls at the waist of a passing stranger

and I separate the label from my beer—

pick pieces off and leave them

on the bar top.

He smiles as he stands, hand
held loosely in the other man's hand—

What has fear done for you?

I open my mouth, but
he's walking farther into the bar—
disappearing into crowds
of people dancing close,
breathing each other's breath.

ON THE BRIDGE

Subraj Singh

I flicked the lit cigarette away, my heart burning, aching, blazing, with guilt and pain and sadness. The cigarette landed in a patch of shrubs on the right bank of the trench, where the tip glowed red for a few seconds before fading away. Fireflies noiselessly flew out of the shrubs and glimmered around the dead cigarette before spreading out over the trees lining both banks of the trench. A few of the insects landed in my hair, where their bodies gently transitioned from coal-black to bright-gold. I combed them out with my fingers and returned to my scattered thoughts.

I thought of my mother and father. I thought of my little brother. I thought of my little brother when he would be older, and in school, when the other children would tease him. I thought of my parents again, my typical Caribbean parents and the typical Caribbean environment they lived in, and the shame they would feel. I thought of them all, separated from me.

I started to think of what would happen to me if people found out, but then I stopped myself. It will not come out. No one would ever know. I ran my fingers through my hair, nervously this time, and looked out at the stretch of placid water before me. The trench lay smooth and serene, like a sleeping snake, stretching itself lazily under the star-strewn sky. The water was dark and calm, smelling of that blackwater scent that we associate with loose, black earth and moss-green weeds and sweet escapades in sugar-cane fields.

The moon was not to be seen that night; it was hidden, watching me from behind a cloud, and yet the silver moonbeams managed to shine down on me. All the light was making me uncomfortable.

I eyed the steeple of the church, in the distance, rising above the trees—a pointing shaft showing the way to heaven. I thought about the long, clean white rows of the church and I thought about the high altar, shrouded in golden cloth, and I thought about my father up there, being everyone else's father, every Sunday. I turned away from the sight of the steeple.

I rubbed the stubble on my chin, thoughtfully, trying to force myself to remember my lines, but I just couldn't do it. Was I nervous? *Yes*. Was I scared? *Absolutely terrified.*

I looked at my watch and realized that he was very late. I had been sitting there for about fifteen minutes, on that mound of old wood and earth, looking over that trench, trying to get my thoughts together. The silent body of water below me also seemed to be waiting. The stillness of it was somewhat disturbing. The black water had a strange sort of tranquility, as if it wanted to burst from the weight of silence that engulfed everything. The silence stretched up towards me, invitingly, luring me in, making me feel as if I should leap from the bridge and sink easily into the dark waters below and yet, at the same time, the black water scared me. It put images of *water-moomas* and fresh-water snakes into my mind.

The night's cold breeze danced around me, tugging at my shirt collar, pulling me, prodding me, harassing me. I wrapped my arms around myself and looked up into the sky, flecked with stars, glinting like stolen diamonds. A dark cloud sailed sleepily above me and I prayed

102

it wouldn't rain now. I looked around the deserted place again and shivered. Out of the corner of my eye I could still see the church's steeple, winking in the starlight at me.

I made up my mind to leave when I finally heard him, walking slowly on the bridge towards me. I nervously looked around, for what was probably the hundredth time that night, but everything was the same—dark trees hiding the trench and the bridge from the nearest street; the steeple probingly visible above the line of trees; the moonless, dark-clouded sky; fireflies fireflying.

It was almost like the first time again. I had been on the same bridge, as scared then as I was now; the night was as silvery as this night was, and the river just as black and motionless, just as serpentine. He looked as he always did. Everything was the same, but it wasn't the same, not really. My hands shivered at my sides, and the light from the stars placed the entire bridge and trench and me and him in a spotlight of the night. The trench lingered beneath my swaying feet, just waiting to reach up and snatch me in its jaws, and I'm sure there were eyes all, all around. I knew it; I felt it. I couldn't believe I had gotten myself into this situation. Truly, I couldn't.

"David," he said, head cocked to one side, eyes large and luminous, a light smile on his face that told me immediately that he was cautious, but happy to see me.

"Yeah," I said, my voice hoarse and faint over the wisps of wind that snatched at it, "Come, siddown."

I patted the space next to me and he delicately sat down, dangling his feet over the bridge's edge and letting them sway over the water the way mine did. The breeze whistled through the holes and cracks in the bridge, occasionally interrupting the thick stillness that lay between us like an invisible, steel curtain. I looked over at him, tall and slim, black hair so long it fell into his eyes, skin so dark it gleamed out of the silver night, like an opal glinting in a sea of black diamonds. I loved his skin. He was wearing jeans and a blue t-shirt. I looked at the shirt with disdain. It was very tight.

"Tell me about the bridge," he said after a while, making a pathetic attempt at conversation while looking around at what really was a mere skeleton of a bridge. I didn't say anything. He already knew everything there was to know about this place. He could hear the age of the bridge in the way it groaned every time anyone walked over it, and he could feel the countless myths that arose around the dead-silence that always seemed to envelop the place.

The bridge. Originally constructed to link the slaves, and later, the Indian immigrants, to the cane-fields where they worked; connecting the opposing worlds of home and hard-work, comfort and calloused hands, beauty and broken-backs. I sat right in the middle of this lost piece of history and looked at him. He didn't like the bridge, or the water, or the wildness of this place, but still he came. Still he came.

Before I knew it, I was looking at his shirt again, and I wondered how on earth he could have walked all the way here in that. It was so very tight. I really hated it.

"You angry with me?" he asked, cutting into my thoughts and smiling slightly again, before looking up into the odd, shapeless cloud that was still suspended over us.

"I know you're angry," he continued, "I know I shouldn't have, but when I saw you there, outside the hospital, I thought you were alone and... I dunno, I was just glad to see you, during the day, in some place that wasn't a cheap hotel room. I don't think it was a big deal. I only said *hi*."

He looked at me again, eyes wide under the shade of dark hair, waiting for a response. I was glad that it was night, so I didn't have to see my own reflection whenever I looked into his eyes. I only saw darkness.

I had practiced the words many times, but nothing came out now. I said nothing and sat there, as immobile as the trench in front of us. He shook his feet nervously and rubbed his hands together either because he was so tense or because the breeze was so cold.

My throat was dry, but I had to say something. "Look," I began, my voice several pitches lower than normal, "You can say hi, but be careful of the way you say it. You don't have to jump around and smile at me like that, like a fool. You know how many people were looking at you?"

"David, I was just happy to see you—"

"And don't talk to me in public if you're not dressed properly," I continued, not waiting to hear him whine, "You're always in those tight clothes, and then there's the black nail polish and all that kinda crap."

He looked away from me. He pressed his lips together and frowned down at the part of the trench that gleamed between his feet. I wondered if he was going to cry. He looked up at me, brimming with sadness, before turning away and whispering bitterly, "You might not realize it, but all those things about me that you're always complaining of, they're the very reasons why you're into me."

I watched him coldly. He stared back at me, refusing to lower his eyes. He stared back at me, bold as never before. I looked into his eyes and I saw him. Eighteen years old, only child, a Linguistics student at the university. I looked deep into his eyes and suddenly I remembered something—a night, at the hotel; he lay with his head on my chest, right over my heart, whispering in the many languages he knew. I looked at him on the bridge and saw him in that hotel room, reciting Spanish rhymes, singing hushed Arabic ditties, teaching me the French words for *sky, earth, boy, girl, love,* and *hate.*

I saw them all, the offspring of everything we had done together in that hotel room, coming towards us in that instant. I saw the lost children from a Spanish novel I read long ago, climbing out of the trench, like crazed sirens, clambering up the banks, with their nails digging into the soft earth. I saw the *bacha bazi,* those glittering dancing boys from the Middle East, prancing around us on the bridge, causing the old boards to rattle and creak under their weight. I saw tiny men, all with curling moustaches, like little goblins, in neat black suits, waving up at me from under the nearby trees, calling "Monsieur, Monsieur." They all stared at me, waving, and smiling, and calling, and singing, and screaming and screaming and screaming.

I blinked and the images were gone. It was now just me and him. No children, no dancing boys, no goblins, nothing. My heart hammered in my chest, my fists were clenched, and a sharp spasm of uneasiness swept through my body. Beads of sweat trickled down my neck, sending soft tingling sensations through me. I blinked rapidly and pushed away his hand as he reached for me, concern etched all over his face.

"I think we should end this," I said, the words I had memorized finally tumbling out of my mouth, "I wanted to meet you tonight to tell you this; I don't want to see you anymore. The way you behaved the

106

other day made me realize that I can't be taking any chances. I thought we could work something out just now, but you obviously don't want to change, or maybe people like you can't change. In any case, I'm seeing someone else now. A girl." It was a lie and I said it because I knew it would hurt him. There was no girl—not yet anyway. I took a deep breath and waited for his reaction.

Tears welled up in his eyes, and he reached for me again, grabbing my arm. "Please," he said, pressing his fingers deep into my arm as I tried to pull away. "Please. . ." he said again, pulling me by the sleeve towards him. He pressed his face to my shoulder and I could feel the flutter of his eyelashes batting away tears. It was disgusting. I tried to ease my body away from him, but he still held my arm tight and did not let go.

"Stop it," I muttered, trying to pry myself from his grip once more, "Stop."

He propped his chin stubbornly on my shoulder and looked steadily at me, tears running down both sides of his face. I was about to shrug him off when it happened. Before I could move another inch, he placed both of his hands around my head and pulled me down into a swift kiss. Our lips touched and I pulled away, knowing that I couldn't ruin that which had taken me so much courage to do. He grabbed the collar of my shirt and pulled my mouth over his again. I felt his lips slip over mine and I sensed a soft murmur rising up from deep within me. His tongue entered my mouth and I started to kiss him fiercely, as my mind screamed madly in revolt. He clambered over me and sat in my lap, ankles locked safely behind my back. I broke away from his mouth and my tongue slid smoothly down his Adam's apple and he clutched my hair in his hands, pulling me down on to him.

Suddenly, something splashed in the water beneath us and I snapped out of the trance. I saw him, wrapped around my body, the heat rising in his face. He looked at me, gloomy and tear-stained, and cupped my face in his hands. Something changed in that moment. My heart rate increased and my palms grew sweaty. I looked around quickly and felt the spasm of fear streak through my body once more.

Without thinking, I quickly spun him around so that he was now facing the open trench, instead of me. I wrapped my legs firmly around his struggling body, and held him tightly against me. Before he could do anything else I hooked my right arm firmly around his neck and held it in place with my other arm. I started to squeeze, putting every ounce of strength I had into closing off his airway. I gripped his throat firmly, constricting it until I felt the veins rising in my arms. He clutched the arm around his neck and tried to scratch and pummel it off of himself. He twisted in agony and pushed in every direction he could, scratching at my face, trying to get me off, making muffled sounds that could have been unborn screams or pleas.

I felt like a god. I squeezed tighter and tighter, and I started to enjoy the way his body wobbled in a mad frenzy against mine. The scratches to my arm and face seared in the cold breeze, but I loved the feeling of the wind licking my wounds. His tears trickled on to me, on to him, into the trench, plopping heavily as though they were drops of blood. He kept struggling to fight me off, trying to gasp for air, his body wriggling, with less and less force in every passing minute. I felt powerful. I hugged him tightly around his throat and felt my body react to the experience.

108

He was pressed so close to me; he was completely in my control. My manhood stiffened against him as I pressed my lips to his temple, as the movement of his body died down, as the ticking of the pulse in his neck died away, as his blood froze in his veins, as the last breath of life squeezed itself from his mouth, as his hands fell to the side. He sagged forwards in my arms, his dark hair framing his face, his eyes still open— but unseeing, unable to ever stare at me again. I pulled him upwards and let his head fall across my shoulder, so his blank gaze extended to the stars above. I dragged my tongue across his cheek, savouring the salty sweetness of him one last time. I pressed my nose to his neck, smelling the musk of his body one final time. I looked at him and felt as though this was the first time I was truly ever seeing him —beautiful and delicate—for what he was. Mine.

I saw the headlights of a car blazing down the nearest street, lighting the tops of the trees as it went flying past us, illuminating the church steeple briefly, but I wasn't scared. The trees kept us safely out of sight. I wasn't scared anymore. No one ever came to the bridge. I wasn't scared at all. No one would ever know.

We stayed there together for a while, him in my arms, eyes open, lips parted, as though reading the skies. I hugged him tightly and hummed one of the Arabic melodies he had taught me. The fireflies were all gone now, and the moon was still not to be seen. By the time my song was finished, it was well after midnight. I gave him one last kiss, gently pushed him into the trench, and started to walk in the direction of the steeple that stood like an inland lighthouse, guiding me home to my parents and my little brother. On the way there all I could think about was the easy grace with which he slid off the bridge, falling with his arms neatly at his sides, his legs turned at splendid angles, his hair billowing out into the breeze, only to be swallowed up by the trench, that silent snake that guarded the bridge.

AN ENCOUNTER IN DOWNTOWN VANCOUVER, CANADA

Amanda Rodriguez

The world is an

Ugly, hateful womb

Hostile to this

Soft naked love.

Two women with

Short hair

Not daring to

Hold hands

Are clocked.

The flight of a fist.

The sizzle of spit.

Through locked teeth

The word *fags*

Thrust from his lips.

Only gravity

Holds me

Inside this body.

Worst of all,

I feel lucky.

Lucky I walked
Away at all.

Lucky I lived to
Hide another day.

NEVER, EVER BRING THIS UP AGAIN

Randi Triant

We were driving in the night in the north of Holland and Dutch Boy needed to make another pit stop.

"Gott verdomme!" Eva muttered. This wasn't like her. She never lost her patience. She never cursed. But we needed to get where we were going and Dutch Boy's repeated need for a bathroom was slowing us down. Driving made him nervous. The Jenever gin he'd been drinking wasn't helping. Eva was strung out from his repeatedly reaching from the back seat through the two front bucket seats and stabbing the play button on her tape deck with his stubby index finger so we could hear once again Peter Gabriel's "So." That's at least what I told myself was the reason she wasn't acting like herself.

"Stop drinking so much," I suggested to Dutch Boy. I was nineteen and full of helpful suggestions. Sometimes it amazed me how little supposed adults knew. I often felt as if everyone else in my life was in a snow globe and I was there to shake them up and the snow would come down as expected again and again. See? I'd say. I told you so.

It was boiling in the Citroën even with the heavy rubber ceiling flap thrown back to let in passing air. Holland had been hit with a weird heat wave in the middle of March. The car smelled of stale tobacco and Jenever gin and Chanel No. 5, Eva's perfume, and something else—a not-unpleasant mixture of patat frites and sweat.

Reaching again from the back seat, Dutch Boy punched the replay button on the tape deck. Eva let out another frustrated moan next to me and clicked her tongue against the roof of her mouth. It was supposed to sound chastising, but it came across as sexy.

We had to be at Den Helder for the nine-thirty ferry, the last one that would leave for Texel, one of the Frisian Islands off the northern coast. It was 9:05 PM and I'd just seen a sign that we were still twenty miles away.

Eva was my father's girlfriend, well, really his fiancée, but I wasn't ready to admit that yet. What daughter doesn't see the new stepmother as a threat?

But that's not the whole story. Not really.

Besides being my future stepmother, Eva was also Dutch Boy's ex-wife, fall-out from her falling in love with my father. And as of last night, she was my lover too, although I'm not sure that having silent sex in a guest room at Dutch Boy's Amsterdam apartment exactly qualifies us as being lovers.

I knew I was in trouble ten months ago, the first time my father had Eva and I meet in a cramped Italian restaurant in Beacon Hill, the tiny size of which made me feel her presence, her closeness, her knees slightly touching mine under the table, as a shudder each time she moved. It was hard not to stare at her long white blond hair expertly wrapped in a bun on top of her head, a beautiful, wooden chopstickey thing through the center, the wisps falling gently around her long neck. It was as if a swan had become human. Eva had a tiny half-moon scar on her left cheek that she said she couldn't remember how she got. You wanted to touch that half moon. She looked taller than she actually was because she always stood or sat with perfect posture, something none of my college friends or I did. She'd been a ballet dancer in a small company in Holland. She'd been married to Dutch Boy, the son of a famous Dutch filmmaker, for five years when she met my father.

Before the Beacon Hill dinner, my father had shown me a photo of her around my age: soft-looking jodhpurs, tall black riding boots. She was on a horse that would've knocked over every table in the small restaurant we were in. This photo had stuck in my mind and immediately gelled into my lasting perception of her: she was a wealthy, beautiful girl who had done all the things a wealthy child does, like taking riding lessons, wearing jodhpurs. Sporting mysterious scars. But although most of those things were true, she hadn't been wealthy. She was a nurse—that's how she'd met my father. Actually, she'd been my *mother's* nurse in the States while on some fellowship studying the mental health of patients post kidney transplant. My mother was at the end of the road in her treatment. She had had a transplant that was kaput. She needed a live-in nurse. Eva needed a place to stay. She was there to make whatever time my mother had left more comfortable. My mother was there because she couldn't be anywhere else.

The first thing Eva had said to me after my father had introduced us in the doorway of that Beacon Hill restaurant was, "We must like each other for your father's sake." She whispered it in my ear, like a come-on.

"Always looking out for someone else," my mother would comment sarcastically when I'd report back to her later about the dinner. "She should worry less about your father and more about me. Your father will manage just fine. He always has." My mother was in her angry period then. The transplant was like a too-tight sweater gift: she couldn't return it. She simply had to live with it as long as she could, knowing it would never be the right fit.

When she said that I was sitting next to her on the hospital bed that Eva had convinced my father to order and have delivered to the house the month before. My mother turned on her side away from me then and told me she was tired.

As we sat down at the table in the restaurant, my father said, "My girls," grinning as if Eva and I were both his daughters, the same age, though she was ten years older.

Now, my father was supposed to be here in the Citroën with Eva and Dutch Boy and me, but he was sitting on a runway at O'Hare. He'd been at a technology conference and due to an engine malfunction was stuck in the plane's first class. I hoped that the endless stream of scotches would do zilch for his frustration at not being here with us. I hoped that he was seated next to a mother and her newborn screaming infant. I hoped he'd be stranded in that plane for days. Somehow in my mind it had become my father's fault that Eva and I had slept together the night before. If he had been here, none of it would have happened. I would've been on the couch and she and my father would have been the ones having the silent sex in the guest room.

This thought made me feel slightly queasy. I cracked open my car window. Not too much though. I couldn't chance it. In my lap was an urn, plain as a coffee pot, as my mother had wished, filled with her ashes. My mother hadn't asked for much in her relatively short life of forty-two years, but the two things she *had* asked for—a faithful husband and to have her remains thrown by him and me in the North

Sea precisely on the ides of March—weren't happening. Not if we didn't get to the ferry in time. I pushed down on the gas pedal.

* * *

By a process of elimination, I'd been picked to drive although I'd never driven before in a foreign country, where I was finding it easy to speed because Holland is flat and everyone speeds in Holland. Eva had night blindness and Dutch Boy was too drunk.

"Milly, we cannot let him drive," Eva had whispered to me when she handed me the keys. There was always a media frenzy attached to anything Dutch Boy did because of his family name, she told me. A DUI for him would have been six o'clock news for months. Which put me and the urn behind the wheel of the Citroën. The urn was my responsibility. I certainly wasn't going to give it to either of them to hold.

With or without my father I was still going to the Dutch island that my mother had stipulated in her will (her mother had been Dutch and was buried there) and I would throw the ashes overboard just as she wished. Meeting my mother's wishes halfway was better than nothing at all. My father had blown the faithfulness part, with the very nurse who had taken care of her, but I would hold up my end. With or without him.

As luck would have it, Eva happened to be in Amsterdam this week also, visiting Dutch Boy. She'd taken care of my mother for ten straight months and needed, according to my father, to see Dutch Boy before she married my father. When I'd questioned him about what he thought of his new wife seeing her ex-husband before the ink was dry on the marriage license my father said, "The Dutch see things differently. They don't hold grudges like we do." He'd insisted that I call Eva as soon as I landed in Amsterdam. Had slipped me an international phone card with her phone number. He'd made it too easy. Like he wanted it to happen.

* * *

"Never, ever bring this up again," Eva said in the car, "but…" Her voice trailed off into one of the drive-by flashes of the white electric windmills spinning outside the windows in the distance.

Dutch Boy said something in rapid Dutch to her.

"Don't do that," Eva snapped.

"What, don't do what?" I said, swerving the car a bit when I looked at her. The wind had been steadily picking up. It felt like it was trying to tell us to turn back. I could barely keep the little car on the road.

"Hey-hey. Watch it." Eva hooked her thumb toward the back seat. "Him. I hate that he does that."

"What—what did he say?"

"Nothing," Dutch Boy said. "I said nothing. It is because I did not say it in English, yes?" It wasn't a question. Dutch Boy always tacked an extra yes on the end of his sentences.

"He told me not to play this game," Eva said.

"Game?"

"Never, ever bring this up again."

"It is a game," Dutch Boy explained, "which my family used to play on trips to pass the time. She says something she has never told anyone

118

before, a secret, and once she says it we are not allowed to speak about it, to ask any questions, yes?" Dutch Boy said.

"Never, ever bring this up again," Eva began again, only this time she plowed on, not letting anything hang in limbo. "I hate nursing."

"What?" I said. "Why—"

The back of my head was slapped. Hard.

"No kicking, no spitting, no diving," Dutch Boy said.

"This is stupid. I mean, why say it if we can't talk—" Another slap. Harder than the first one.

"Your serve, gringa," Dutch Boy said. Eva had told me he'd spent a lot of time in Cuba, trying to forget who he was and who he was related to. He liked to throw in Spanish words along with sports references that sounded strange coming out of his mouth.

"Stop hitting me," I yelled at him. "Why isn't it your turn? Why don't *you* go?"

My fingertips were shaking on the steering wheel. Ever since I'd slept with Eva I felt that things might unravel at any moment. I mean, if *that* had happened, what else could? How far were we from the ferry now, I wondered? I placed my left hand on top of the urn nestled between my legs. It calmed me down a little.

"He never goes," Eva told me, sighing. "That is why our marriage failed."

"Well, that's just stupid," I said. "Your marriage failed because you were sleeping with my father."

"It is more complicated than that," Eva said. Dutch Boy in the backseat mimicked Eva's clicking tongue sound.

Glancing sideways, I saw her push down on the chopstickey thing, sending it deeper into the soft web of her hair. Last night her hair had been down and I was surprised by its length past her shoulders, by its softness. By my fingers wrapping strands of it round and round.

"It all seems pretty simple to me. You fucked my father and at the same time fucked *him*," I said, trying to hurt her and hooking my thumb towards the back seat like she had. But she only sighed and looked out her window.

"I know why you say these things," she murmured. Immediately, I felt ashamed, any feeling of having bested her shriveling under the weight of my wanting to please her.

"Before you enter the game you must be prepared to play, yes?" Dutch Boy whispered in my ear. I could smell the Jenever on his breath. The overpowering smell of rye and juniper berries. The type of smell you either loved or didn't. There was no in-between. Like so many Dutch things: the flatness and wide horizon that made you feel small and big at the same time, the mayonnaise they globbed on their patat frites, so sweet and so unhealthy, their wooden shoes. Shoes that hurt your feet, but you had the urge to skip in them.

"Your turn, little miss American princess," Dutch Boy said, falling back against his seat.

When we'd met the night before at his house, I'd immediately liked Dutch Boy in that way that you adore everyone you meet in a European country when you're nineteen, but apparently not, I was fast realizing, when he was drunk.

"Why should I play—" Another cuff to the back of my head. "Shit, stop hitting me. I'm going to get us into an accident."

Now it was Eva's turn to say something in Dutch. She'd swiveled around and leaning through the two front seats, practically spat the words into Dutch Boy's face and then slapped him on the side of the head.

"Ow," Dutch Boy said.

"Could everyone stop hitting each other?" My voice was a whiney ten-year-old's.

Eva faced forward again. "He is jealous that I am giving you too much attention. Ignore him."

I watched Dutch Boy in the rearview, massaging his left cheek. He was handsome in a nonchalant way. Despite the hot weather, he was wearing a trench coat that made him look like James Dean: wide-set eyes married with high cheekbones and pillowy lips. I thought of chocolate pudding when I looked at those lips. The top part of his face was all strength and determination, the bottom all gentleness and softness. I could understand why Eva had fallen for him years ago. Maybe if my father had arrived on time, I wouldn't have ended up in bed with Eva. I would've ended up in Dutch Boy's master bedroom. I felt woozy again. The three of us in this car were like one of those blackboard logic equations in high school that spiral on and on, row after row, words tumbling over words, stumbling their way through deduction to clarity. *Three gods A, B, and C are called, in no particular order, True, False, and Random. True always speaks truly, False always speaks falsely, but whether Random speaks truly or falsely is a completely random matter. Your task is to determine the identities of A, B, and C by asking three yes/no questions.* The interpretations were infinite. More often than not my questions were wrong. They never added up quite right. There was always a fatal break in my reasoning.

By now we were ten miles outside of Den Helder. Instead of flat nothingness, you could see in the bright moonlight a darkened farmhouse here and there. Another twenty electric windmills flashed by, their moving whiteness glowing in the dark like waving human arms, flagging us down to stop. Maybe we'd get there in time. Maybe I could avoid this whole never, ever business. What would I say anyway? Which never, ever would I bring up? There were so many.

"Never, ever bring this up again," Dutch Boy said quietly from the back seat. "I am ashamed that I do not understand my father's films. I try and nothing. Just people doing boring things. My father is ashamed of me for this too. Please, do not look at me, Milly. Watch the road. We will get in an accident, yes?"

Eva turned around in her seat again, only this time, reaching out, she cradled his face in both of her hands, murmuring Dutch.

"Hey, I thought you said we shouldn't do that," I said peevishly to the rearview mirror.

Eva faced forward. "We should not do a lot of things, Milly, but we do them anyway." She was staring out her window, but I knew she wasn't being philosophical, wasn't simply waxing eloquent, as my mother would've said. I felt woozy again. Did she mean we shouldn't have done what *we* did, but it was okay that we did it because we *had* to do it? Or did she mean that we shouldn't have done what we did, period? I thought of that blackboard equation again. I'd hated my logic teacher, hated his rambling that you got you lost five minutes in, hated his all-too-visible naiveté that all the students took advantage of. One day, whenever he turned his back to write something on the board, a couple of kids snuck out the back classroom door. By the end of the class, more than half of the students were missing. He seemed at first baffled by the empty chairs, but then I watched as he, with a shake of his head, appeared to question himself as to whether the chairs had actually ever been filled. Like it was all a hallucination. Made-up. A dream.

As we finally passed a sign that said *Den Helder 5 km*, I wondered if it was the logic itself I hated, the equations that I could never wrap my head around. I had been out of my depth. It was as simple as that. Who liked being on shifting ground?

My father had told me once that the reason he'd started the affair with Eva was that she took him "out of his element." What did that mean exactly? Did that mean he, unlike me, liked the uncertainty of uncharted territory? He liked flailing around in the dark? Liked the tingly sense of waiting for his outstretched hands to land on something familiar? The free fall of it all?

There had been nothing familiar about being with Eva the night before. It'd started out innocently enough. Doesn't it always, I could hear my mother's voice saying. Now who's being naïve? One night, right before the end, I'd been sitting with my mother and she'd caught me watching Eva too closely as she'd walked out of my mother's bedroom after bringing her her cyclosporine and a glass of milk. She'd told me before that the cyclo tasted like she was swallowing a metal can.

"You're always so impressionable," my mother muttered as she watched me watch Eva leave. "But with the wrong things. Life isn't as colorful as you think."

I think she was wrong about that.

In Dutch Boy's guest room the night before, there had been two twin beds. When I came in from washing up in the bathroom, Eva was pushing the two beds together.

"This is better," she said, laughing. She brushed the wisps out of her eyes. "Slumber party."

After she'd turned out the light, her arm came to rest across my chest, her fingers lightly touching my neck.

"You miss your mother." It wasn't a question. More like an observation without any hint of accusation. Something about that made me want to weep. I hadn't cried at my mother's funeral. Not because I didn't love her. I loved her too much. If the boy in the Dutch children's story pulls his finger out of the dike, the flood will come. Don't cry, don't cry, I'd repeated to myself at the beginning of her funeral, but then I didn't have to as whatever sadness I'd felt was washed away with embarrassed disbelief and then anger as the service went on. First, the pastor gave a dull, generic description of the woman he so obviously hadn't known, and then my father, unmoored without my mother's sickly presence justifying his new life with Eva, slowly made his way to the lectern and recited far too many intimate stories about my mother that shouldn't have been mentioned at all, yet alone in public. My mother would have hated every bit of it. Any desire to cry flew out those church doors along with any good will towards my father that I might have had.

In bed, I tucked my face into Eva's neck and that was that. Before I knew what was happening I was crying. Sobbing really.

"You are just like her," Eva whispered in my ear. "So beautiful. So hard on the outside, but soft, like a turtle, on the inside." She called me

124

zeeschildpadcha—turtle but with the cha on the end, a form of Dutch endearment. She'd taught me that during the Italian dinner with my father.

"Vlindercha," she'd said in the restaurant, slipping a pasta bow tie gleaming with oil into her mouth. "Little butterfly."

Now, the mention of turtle made me cry harder. My mother had collected turtles. Lots of them. Glass and silver and porcelain. In mid-stream crawls. With babies on their hard back. Perched everywhere around the house on shelves and on bookcases. As a child I'd found one in the freezer, forgotten, an accident waiting to shatter into a hundred pieces.

Then, what started as tenderness on Eva's part—her fingers touching my face, then softly rubbing my bare arm, moving up under my t-shirt sleeve to massage my shoulder—all of that tenderness quickly turned into me pulling her closer and me finding her lips, in the dark, in the unknown territory of us.

* * *

In the morning, when I awoke, she was gone. Already up and out as my mother would've said, which always reminded me of a radio controller saying over and out. Eva's absence startled me. For a few minutes I actually thought she'd still be there, maybe asleep, maybe propped up on an elbow, watching me, a smile on her face. Or no, maybe not a smile. Maybe a troubled look as she would've spent the whole night awake, worried about how we'd let my father down gently.

But none of that happened. Not the smile or the look of concerned worry. Not the telling my father. She was gone.

In the shower I kept dropping the soap. Every time I thought I had a firm grasp on it and was sliding it over a thigh or an arm, suddenly it would launch and hit the shower's tiled floor with a thud. After the fourth time of dropping it, I slid it back on the soap dish.

Maybe Eva had left Dutch Boy's house in the middle of the night, as soon as I'd fallen asleep. How could I do what I needed to do with my mother's ashes with only Dutch Boy? Maybe she was on her way right now to a telephone booth, where she'd call my father and tell him that I had done the unspeakable: I'd manipulated her into having sex with me. Had worked her, taken advantage of her compassion and sympathy. She was just offering me what she'd given all of her dying patients' families: comfort and a bit of kindness. She was my father's mistress, his soon-to-be wife, my mother's one-time sworn enemy, and finally my mother's savior when the pain became unbearable and all she wanted was Eva, the winged deliverer of morphine. Not me. Not my father. Wasn't that enough? Why had I done it?

Now, up ahead there was a line of traffic.

"It's only thirty kilometers speed here, yes?" Dutch Boy said anxiously.

"I cannot believe we made it," Eva said and pushed in the lighter. She'd given up smoking two months ago. "Slow down, Milly. You are scaring him."

A man in a blue uniform waved us on, into the tight parking area on board the ferry. When we parked on the lowest level of the ferry, I watched in the rearview mirror Dutch Boy's panicking face as a car pulled up very close behind us and parked. Cars were three deep on either side of us. Now someone was pulling in back of the person in back of us. I knew what Dutch Boy was thinking. It was the same thing I was thinking: How would we ever get out in an emergency?

Eva and Dutch Boy opened their doors.

"Coming?" Eva asked me.

"I need something to drink, yes? A bar, I think," Dutch Boy said. As he walked fast in between our car and the one in front, I could see his face was flushed in the ferry lights.

"He doesn't like boats," Eva said quietly. "He thinks we'll drown."

"Why did he come then?"

She shrugged. "For me." She turned to me in the car. "And I came for you. And you came for your mother."

"And dad didn't come at all."

She got out of the car, but then ducked her head back inside.

"Your father is here, trust me. You are him and he is you."

We found Dutch Boy on the top deck, his trench coat collar turned up against the wind, his right hand wrapped tightly around a half-full beer stein. It was chilly up here. A cooler wind was moving in, picking up moisture from the North Sea, our faces reddening from the wind licking.

The boat's horn let out that lonesome ship sound, that hollow, bottomless, basso profundo that wallops you in the stomach and simultaneously travels down and up your body, leaving emptiness in its path. The ferry began to move quickly now, the dock being lost in the wake.

I put the urn on top of the railing. My right hand rested on the lid. It trembled slightly.

Dutch Boy put his now empty beer stein down on the deck and standing up, folded his hands in front of his trench coat, against his stomach. He closed his eyes, bowing his head, like a pastor.

Eva slipped her arm around my shoulders. It felt like the basso profundo. I gripped the urn tighter with both hands.

"Never, ever bring this up again," I shouted so they could hear me over the wind, the ferry. Dutch Boy's eyes opened, startled by my yelling. I felt Eva's hand slide off and watched her mouth form the start of a word. I knew she knew. I took the lid off the urn and along with the ash that spiraled skyward and out to sea, my words streamed out, cutting Eva's off, taking the life out of the air around us and propelling us on through uncharted waters.

CHRYSALIS

Sam Gray

Cup my breasts so tight
they flatten into lungs,
into my lungs that struggle to inhale.
Tighter, tighter conceal the mounds
that signify '*lifebearer.*'
Make me pass '*lifegiver,*'
if only for the hour, from the corner
of their eyes.

Cup my groin
(how masculine)
and pretend there's something there.
My outward pleasure kept inward
and sacred.
(pretend)
Oh you must feel it
pulsating this wildly inside myself!
(I beg of you)

Cup my swollen cheeks with black and blue.
Irises illuminate the shock of sunlight
I almost never filter. Tremble
with me. Find the place inside yourself

to feel my misplaced passions, strip
yourself until we can hide blatantly,
so naked to become invisible.

Promise not to be afraid
of who I will become.

A BLIZZARD OF SOLITUDE

J L Homan

As I climbed the stairs exiting the stage door of the New York State Theatre, the storm hit me almost joyously; sparkling and gusting horizontally. Fortunately, my folding umbrella was in my backpack, along with my usher's uniform. My walk uptown would be a concerto with these wintry, whirling white elements fighting against me, and I imagined performing the "Dance of the Snowflakes" from Balanchine's Nutcracker. I loved the city at times like this.

Everyone knew the first blizzard of the year was forecast but, in fact, this nor'easter was worse than predicted. Audiences tumbled out into sizeable snowdrifts on Lincoln Center's plaza from the Metropolitan Opera and Avery Fisher Hall as well as those attending the New York City Ballet's performance I had just worked.

Most intrepid New Yorkers had bundled up in anticipation of the storm, knowing that their journeys home would be challenging, but few were as prepared as they wished they'd been. As violent northwesterly winds blew this blizzard across the plaza, the Center's Revlon Fountain became almost indistinguishable, covered by drifts already two feet high.

Those New Yorkers who hadn't been intimidated by the forecast now found themselves, like me, almost enjoying the battle of the elements. People helped each other in and out of cabs and over the snow drifts that held cars hostage against the curbs. Buses crept along their designated routes as their passengers stared out the frosty windows, with looks of wonder as well as worry.

I headed uptown into the gusts, trying to maintain an opened umbrella and realizing that this trek to my fifth-floor walk-up apartment would take longer than usual. But what did that matter? As Balanchine's "Serenade" was replaying in my mind, I really didn't care. Tchaikovsky's score added a magical, musical dimension to the evening's inclement elements.

Crossing West 72nd Street, I heard a friendly male voice from behind me gasp, "Hello! Are you enjoying the evening?"

"I love this! Isn't it beautiful?" I shouted, trying to be heard above the traffic and howling winds.

"You have an interesting idea of beauty, young man," he added, almost unable to speak between gusts.

"Hello, my name is Jaime. Hey, it's not one of those greedy golf umbrellas, suitable for a family of four, but I'm willing to share it, if you'd like."

With our heads bowed behind the small umbrella, we headed into the savage winds blowing down Broadway. The gale forces smacked our little, black shield, while whipping up our clothing and stinging our cheeks. I noticed that he was wearing shiny patent leather shoes. This handsome, middle-aged, gentleman was dressed formally. His white silk scarf would not stay tucked inside his dress coat and he was hugging a violin case.

"No one was expecting anything this bad!" he yelled and then added, "How far are you going?"

His question interrupted my imagining Carrie Pepperidge in *Carousel* singing *His name is Mr. Snow*—**and** he looked like Stanley Tucci in a tuxedo. I responded, "How far would you like me to go?"

He laughed.

"I live on 90th, between West End and Riverside Drive, across the street from Shirley Verrett," I said.

"Oh, you're into opera? I play with the Metropolitan Opera Orchestra." Between gusts, he explained that he lived on West 77th and asked, "Would you like to stop in before continuing your trek uptown? I'll make some tea."

Being picked up by a man in formal wear amidst this raging snowstorm seemed positively cinematic. As we rounded the corner of West 77th and reached the canopy of his building, the howling winds became somewhat quieter. He extended his hand and said, "Hi, I'm Ernie. Come on up."

Don't you agree that first contact, even if only shaking hands in gloves, can be indelibly memorable? The movie in my mind was developing in an interesting way, and it had nothing to do with Carrie Pepperidge, Mr. Snow or *Carousel*. Where will this story end, I wondered, almost aloud, but then caught myself.

Right on track, Ernie kissed me soon after we entered his apartment, and for much longer than I think either of us expected. I reeled a bit, not from surprise but from his cold, luscious yet tender lips. We jokingly agreed that it was a good sign neither of us had turned into frogs, but then we hadn't used tongues. In my experience a great, or even good, kisser usually indicated other impressive carnal abilities. Carly Simon's "Anticipation" now replaced Rodgers and Hammerstein as the musical underscoring that was running through my mind.

Ernie helped me remove my snow-encrusted backpack, coat, scarf and gloves, and requested that I remove my boots. Then he slipped into a pair of what seemed to be Gucci bedroom slippers, which were patiently awaiting his return like loyal pets. He undid his bow tie, hung his overcoat on a wooden hanger in his front-hall closet, dimmed the lights, lit a few candles and turned on a recording of what sounded like a Schubert Piano Concerto.

Introductions over tea are always very civilized, but rarely this romantic. Entering his living room, I perused all the musical references that lined the walls of his comfortable lair, made all the more charming by candlelight. As he prepared tea in his tiny kitchen, I attempted to relate details of the evening's NYC Ballet program. He was either uninterested or too focused on making tea.

Finally, I asked, "How long have you been with the Met orchestra?"

"Since graduating Juilliard. Let's just say that was some years ago. What do you do?" he inquired.

Now, when this question is asked of any New Yorker, their answer totally defines who that person is—almost like asking their zip code: Social strata, economic resources, gay, straight, single, married with or without two point three children and/or Akitas, New York City's Dog of Distinction throughout the last half of the 1980s.

"Oh, I'm a dancer. I've been on the road with Goodspeed's *Little Johnny Jones* for the last ten months. They gave us the holidays off. We're about to go back into rehearsal for a New York revival opening in March. It'll be my third Broadway show. Mr. Kelly, the NYS Theatre manager, lets me usher when I'm not on the road. I help fill in for ushers who aren't able to make it to work for whatever reason and tonight there were several!"

"A working dancer. That's rather rare."

"Is it?" I laughed nervously.

"Black or white?" he asked. "I mean, how would you like your tea?"

"Light, please, no sugar."

I continued stammering, "I … I'm 34, which I know is old for a dancer, but I'm still cast as a character juvenile. I really don't want to turn forty wearing silly hats and funny ties and, you know, reciting memorable Broadway phrases like, 'Holy Cabooses, Cornelius!' or 'Jeelly-Cly, Professor' while auditioning for my next job."

I wasn't sure Ernie was even listening, which added to my nervousness. So I continued to ramble because, well, it is just easier to tell someone everything about yourself when you're not certain that you'll ever see him again.

"So I'm considering a few options if I choose to cross the footlights," I continued. "Ushering at Lincoln Center is another connection to theatre. I'm really enjoying my introduction not only to NYCB and Balanchine, who has actually taught me to appreciate Stravinsky, but also the New York City Opera."

"Oh, so you enjoy Stravinsky. He can be a challenge for a violinist." He entered carrying a tray with a pot of tea, two mugs, napkins and some small, half-moon-shaped, two-toned biscuits, placing it on the ottoman.

Ernie sat down beside me on his sofa and said, "I'll play mother. There always needs to be a 'mother' when serving tea, or so I was taught. Now, you would like your tea light, no sugar, correct?"

The first few sips of tea were perfectly delicious, a mild Asian blend, just the right strength, and the biscuits smelled of amaretto. As we relaxed into the overstuffed comfort of his sofa, I wondered: Does this thing recline?

Ernie opened the first few studs of his formal shirt, revealing a silky pattern of dark chest hair and my id, ego and superego were immediately riddled with lascivious thoughts: I feared they were flashing across my forehead like daily stock indexes at NYSE.

"Do you live alone?" he asked.

"Yes. Yes, I do. In a fifth-floor walkup." I admitted, setting my tea mug down next to his on the tray atop the ottoman, serving as a coffee table.

I continued, "Two years ago, my partner of six years moved to LA and then decided to never come back. Our careers took different paths … or something like that … being bi-coastal is just too expensive. It gets lonely, especially at night. Do you?"

"I do, now. He moved out after I was diagnosed HIV positive."

The movie playing in my mind was not going to end as I had hoped. The soundtrack underscoring my imagined romance screeched to a stop, like a phonograph needle sliding across a vinyl record, recalling the 63 friends I had already lost to the pandemic. Noticing my awkward silence, he assured me that he had protection and that I shouldn't worry.

Reaching for his tea mug, Ernie broke our silence and asked, "Do you like the tea? I brought it back from our last Asian tour."

"Oh, yes … the tea … the tea is very good. Thank you."
Pause…pause….pause.

"The tea will certainly keep me warm on my way uptown. Only 23 blocks to go and, you know, Ernie, as sexy and as interesting as I find you … and…musical … and kind ... and sexy …. You know, tonight is a 'school night' of sorts and I have to be at a temp job at 8:30 a.m. tomorrow." I stood up.

"I understand …," he said as he stood up. "It's a frightening time in our community, isn't it? And even more frightening being alone."

I hugged him and tried to explain the ubiquitous fears that every gay man in NYC shared, all of which he had heard before. "It only takes once," as the metro and subway posters kept reminding us all. Ernie helped me back into all my winter paraphernalia and opened his apartment door. We kissed goodbye in the cramped hallway of his apartment.

There I was, standing in his doorway, wrapped up like the Michelin logo and realizing I had to go to the bathroom. I mumbled through my scarf, "My therapist believes that anxiety and being alone are inextricably linked, you know … and could be the only two things with which no one, other than yourself, can help you. You know, while others can help you pay taxes and, even, die…," the Freudian slip horrified me more than it did him.

Hoping to disguise my verbal *faux pas*, I added, "For years I've been trying to find a solitude that I'm hoping will alleviate both to some extent. Intimacy *vs.* Anxiety: The most *au courant* of gay dynamics, isn't it?"

"I really wish that you would stay," he stated calmly from his doorway, elegantly disheveled in his chic bedroom slippers. "We don't have to do anything but hold each other."

"I really wish I could, too, but I can't… I'm afraid."

"We're all afraid," he added.

"Thank you and please forgive me." I said, before stepping into the elevator car.

As I began the second leg of my homebound trek, the snowy sparkles now were a little less bright and the wind's bite a little more haunting. I couldn't tell if it was the wind that was making my eyes tear, or my fears and compassion?

Walking up West End Avenue, being pelted as much by snow as by the realization of a shifting world, I wondered if anyone actually has any control over, much less a concept of, the future or solitude.

Ah, blizzards … they have never been the same.

NUCLEAR FAMILIES

Matt Hall

No one gets cancer in my family.

We live forever, long and healthy—

100th birthdays hardly impress.

The early deaths, those few,

Were accidents, heart attacks

Never cancer.

The picture of health—

A meat, a starch, and something green,

For any game, two even teams,

Firefly summers in the yard,

Hearthside winters, playing cards.

Nightly stories, daily prayers,

Backscratch bedtimes, teddy bears-

No dangers, troubles, toils, or snares

til someone dropped a bomb.

Small and deadly, unexpected,

The trap doors of a heart creaked open

And from them, falling, irrevocable—

The words "gay", and also "I'm".

And we have cancer now.

I guess I really should have expected
some radioactive fallout
from nuclear families.

A REAL LOVE

Sari Katharyn

It's been twenty minutes since the wedding was supposed to start. Everything is ready: the cathedral has been adorned, from top to bottom, with delicate arrangements of various peonies, their combined smell almost intense enough to overpower the incense. The light spilling in through the stained glass clerestory windows bathes the altar in a warm glow that I would call holy, if I believed in that. But even if it isn't holy to me, it is at least beautiful. Twenty minutes ago, I would have said it was perfect. But I can't, because the bride isn't here. And neither are you.

No one is willing to look the groom in the eye. I can hear him shifting from foot to foot by the altar, all towering six feet of him a breath away from exploding into a mess of nerves. I don't even remember his name, but I'm sure we're both wishing for the same thing: for his bride to show up, and for her ex to take her seat beside me.

When we arrived half an hour ago, the usher seated us in the first pew, flushed close to the central aisle. I was about to ask you why we were being seated beside the bride's immediate family, when several things happened at once, or in quick succession: the cathedral bells began to ring, signaling the start of the wedding, and your phone began to ring in your pocket. "It's Zin," which meant Zinnia the bride, of course. "I think I have to take this." You weren't frowning, but there was something guarded in your eyes. You didn't wait for my reply, sweeping out the cathedral through a side door, the echoes of the bells ringing like the alarms in my head.

It only took a few minutes for me to start sweating, hoping that the slip I was wearing prevented the perspiration from staining the deep maroon fabric of my skater dress. It was a color we agreed on together, to match your three-piece suit. "We're going to look better than the bride and groom," were your exact words, only two hours ago, as you coiled your hair into a chignon. How did we get from there to here, with me sitting alone in the perfect location for people's viewing pleasure?

When I pull out my phone from my pocket to send you another message, I catch the quick flicker of another stranger's glance sliding away from me. I can't blame them; without you here, I don't belong. Do any of them suspect why you aren't here? And if they do, who do they see when they glance at me? Am I an unwitting damsel in distress in this scenario? A foolish rebound publicly scorned? An unwelcome sinner in the house of their God? A pitiful fourth party in an already crowded triangle? An accomplice to a cruel home wrecker? Is that what you are?

Something about the way people keep looking at me reminds me of myself, the night I met you; maybe it's the same false sense of subtlety I had when I kept glancing at you across the fusion sushi restaurant, in between bites of sashimi and sips of sake. I couldn't help myself; you were an entirely different kind of feast, the ruby red of your floral suit popping out against the background of bland charcoal grey business suits, the dark brown waves of your hair tossed casually over one shoulder, your lips shimmering in the low light when you spoke.

I still remember how I averted my gaze every time your head turned my way, and how relieved I felt when we were formally introduced later that night, sure that I'd gotten away with my ogling. It was only in the morning, when you said, "I'm so glad I decided to meet the girl who kept staring at me on sushi night," that I realized how wrong I was. You said it so casually, while retrieving your creased floral suit from my bedroom floor, that I needed a moment for the words to register. When they finally did, I rolled over to bury my blush into my pillow, while you laughed and asked, "Oh, Rex, did you really think I wouldn't notice?" The mattress dipped under your weight, then your body was over mine, your fingers pressed to my sides, my ribs, tickling me into the sheets. "I liked it," you murmured softly, like a sweet secret, even after I laughed my morning breath into your face. "And I like looking at you, too."

If I had to pick our best hits, that moment would be a strong contender for the top spot, as the first of many domestic mornings, the first of many days starting with the sound of our laughter. It was so easy to fall into something more with you. But it's hard to reconcile the memory of you then with your absence now; if we had bad mornings, I would probably be recalling them instead of that first one, just to see if any of them could have foreshadowed today. But we never had bad mornings, did we? Or even bad afternoons, evenings, nights. Every time we were close to a fight, you pivoted, dousing the charcoals before they turned into flames. I used to think that was a good thing, but now I wonder if that was a sign that things weren't as they seemed. Could you really know someone if you never fought, even lovingly, with them?

I'm tamping down the urge to squirm in my seat when the officiant approaches the groom, and murmurs something softly to him. He isn't the only one murmuring; the low hum in the cathedral that began when the last echo of the bells fell silent seems on the brink of exploding into full-blown chatter. I wonder if anyone else is thinking about standing up and leaving. The children have obviously expended all their patience; there's a young boy seated on the pew across the aisle begging his father to undo his tie. Somewhere behind me, a mother is shushing her baby, trying to contain the whimpering before it escalates. Let the baby cry, I'm tempted to tell her. At least someone will be honest about how they're feeling.

The closest we've ever been to a bad night was the time you told me about this wedding. "Won't it be strange?" I asked cautiously, after you passed me your phone, the wedding invitation on the screen: "Dearest Linnea, Please join us as we exchange our vows" framed by a garland of white roses. You were silent for a moment, before turning your back to me and flicking the stove on. I watched you pour oil into our newly bought wok, waiting for it to heat, then sliding in cubed tofu. "Yes," you admitted, over the low hiss, "But not for the reasons most people might think. Things with us were so bad towards the end. I could never go back to that."

"So why go at all? You could decline the invite and take a trip with me instead."

You held on to your silence longer. I learned early on that this was how you usually were when you talked about Zin; when you revealed your history, it came out in small splinters, in quick bursts. On rare moments, you regurgitated your memories in a jumbled word vomit I couldn't always make out. I didn't always understand why you were so protective of your shared past, until the night you told me about how she insisted, for all those years, on keeping your relationship a secret, from your families and most of your friends. "Old habits are hard to break," you joked, but there was a pain in your eyes I couldn't ignore. So I tried not to pry, to give you as much space and time as you needed to piece together your experiences into something you could talk about. But should I have pried, for your sake as much mine? For Zin's, even? For the groom standing a few feet away from me? Could I have avoided this outcome?

That night, the silence stretched between us, measured by the tofu searing on the stove. I remember staring at the bits of your tattoo peeking out of your contrast tank, a cluster of violets you had inked after your relationship ended. Who were you before you had those flowers on your skin? "She was my best friend for years before we got together." You finally said, as you killed the stove and turned to me, folding your arms over your chest, something almost apologetic in your eyes. "Maybe things will always be strange between us. I can't change that." You paused for a breath, somehow looking smaller. "Is that okay?"

I've revisited that night so many times in my head, imagining all the different results we could have had, if I had been a little more honest with my reply: No, she hurt you, I can't overlook that. No, she never even said sorry, she doesn't deserve you. No, it isn't. Do you still love her? But in the moment, all I could think of was how much it took out of you to ask me that question, how defeated you already seemed, ready for the rejection and the end. I could bear the lie, I decided. "Yes."

I could see the joy in your eyes, even if I couldn't feel it myself. You crossed the distance between us and wrapped me in your arms, and when I leaned my head against your shoulder, I could smell the faint aroma of tofu clinging to your clothes. "Thank you." I felt you hide your face in my shoulder, inhaling shakily, your ribs expanding against mine. I ran a hand down your back, swallowing past the lump in my throat. When you stopped trembling, you turned your lips to my neck. "Come with me to the wedding. Please." I closed my eyes, but hummed in assent anyway, and felt your lips bloom into a smile by my pulse. "I love you," you whispered, pressing your lips against my skin. Do you, really? "So much." More than her?

"Oh, thank God," I hear the groom say, and I twist around to see you at the cathedral doors. Everyone else turns to look, just in time to see you offer your arm to someone I can't see yet, until she slides her arm through yours and steps closer to you. I've never met Zin in person, but she is as beautiful as she is in your pictures together, especially this older and sharper version in a lavender ombré wedding gown. But I don't linger on her long, my gaze returning to you; as you move closer, it's easier to see that your eyes look slightly bloodshot, but nothing else about you looks ruffled or out of place from the moment we arrived. I don't know what that means.

Neither of you even wait for any kind of music to start, beginning your walk up the aisle. The guests rush to their feet, the sudden burst of sound a whiplash compared to the earlier drone. You meet my gaze as soon as I'm within your line of sight, and the smile that spreads across your face produces an acute ache in my chest.

You both stop when you reach the end of the aisle, before the groom steps in, eager to move things along. As soon as the couple begins making their way towards the altar, you take your place in the pew, turn to me, and slide your hand into mine. You sigh with something that sounds like relief. "Hey," you whisper, your eyes never leaving my face, even as we sit for the officiant to begin his opening remarks. "I'm sorry about that. I tried to hurry her, but she had so much to say. Are you okay?"

I didn't realize I was shaking until you held my hand. I want to speak, but if I open my mouth, I think I'll start crying. You must realize that, because you slide closer, letting go of my hand to wrap your arm around me instead, your hold firm and instantly comforting. You bend towards me, until your face is inches from mine.

"I'm so sorry," you whisper, keeping your voice low, to avoid disrupting the ceremony, or to evade invasive ears, I'm not sure. "I didn't think it would take so long. She just wanted to say sorry, for everything. There was so much crying, they had to keep redoing her make-up. Then she asked me to walk her, and I couldn't say no." I press my lips together, and you chuckle. "I know, I know. I just wanted to get it over with. All I could think about was you, sitting here, alone with these people. I'm sorry, Rex." You press a kiss to my temple, not caring who may see or what they may think. "Do you want to leave?" You ask, leaning back to look me in the eye. "We can go."

"Why?" I manage to ask, the ache in my chest subsiding with each breath. I can feel all my worries from the past half hour becoming smaller with you here. Someone begins to read a Bible verse in the background, and it doesn't elude me that neither of us has looked at the altar since the ceremony started. "You really wanted to come."

"I was wrong about what I wanted." You smile again, a tender, private thing. "You were right, let's go on a trip." You must see the surprise on my face, because you chuckle and add, "I think it will be good for us. We've never gone away together."

The groom is just beginning his vows when you help me to my feet. Zin may or may not look our way, neither of us notice, and we may never know. The same guests who kept glancing at me earlier shoot us dirty looks, but you don't care, and I follow your lead and ignore them, too. You take me out the same side door you exited through barely half an hour ago, and in the open air, I feel lighter already, my leftover anxiety giving way to adrenalin. You laugh at my obvious relief, pulling me close to embrace me in the light. It's just you and me now.

It feels real. It feels like another beginning.

LESBIANA

Erika De Jesus Rodriguez

Baby, I've been a tortillera since birth. Marimacho as a kid. An adult descarada wrapped in lace bras and tight jeans. A bilingual femme with a multi-talented tongue, a grip full hand and an immigrant imagination. I've always touched in two places at once. Up high or down low, tu me dices donde me quieres. I'll spoon you in English, riddle you in Spanish. My folks in casa won't approve. "Eso es pecado!" "That's a sin!" They'll shout at us. I won't hear them between your thighs, so keep me safe from senses. You'll fear the repercussions, question if nights of passion are worth the miradas of the morning, but mi amor. It takes nothing to navigate separately, cowardly, out of unowned shame and we're... amor, we're just too brave.

YOU CAME BACK

David K. Slay

It was Ron Cooper's first semester at his local state college, and he was in the cafeteria drinking overly-sugared coffee and smoking while trying to compose a letter. He hadn't acquired a taste for coffee yet, and especially not for smoking in the morning, but that seemed to be what freshmen did, and where they hung out between classes. It was a big room with a high ceiling and mid-morning sunlight streamed in between venetian blinds. A soft blue-gray haze hung in the air and seemed to muffle the sounds of casual conversations mixed with the random clatter of cups and saucers. The letter was to his high school English teacher, from the previous year, to go with a book he was returning. The teacher had taken a special interest in Ron, and had encouraged his creative writing endeavors, so he didn't want the letter to be poorly composed, or to disappoint.

While thinking how to word something, and absentmindedly looking around the room, he saw Stan Wilson, sitting alone, just a few tables away. Stan had been senior class president three years earlier, when Ron was a sophomore in high school. He was reading a textbook propped open on a new leather briefcase, an ashtray on one side and a coffee cup on the other. He had gained a little weight, looked more muscular, but still had the same clean-cut blond hair, except shorter, now in a crew cut. Ron quickly glanced around the room, as when you notice something very unusual, and wonder why no one else sees the same thing. But then he felt silly, realizing Stan wasn't a celebrity for anyone there except him.

Watching Stan absorbed in the book, occasionally underlining something with a pencil, Ron had a vivid recollection of when he first saw him. He was a late-blooming adolescent in his first year of high school, sitting in the grandstands of the football field, and down on the red dirt track, near the finish line for the 100-yard dash, Stan walked up to a chrome microphone on a floor stand, the kind Elvis used on stage. It was an all-school assembly, and several school officials sat in folding chairs on the grass behind him, waiting their turns to speak. A line of cheerleaders and song girls in royal blue and pure white outfits stood at parade rest behind them, pom-poms at their feet. It was a bright fall morning in southern California and he faced the sun in a sky-blue dress shirt and khakis, one hand in a pocket, the other resting lightly on the mike stand. His blond hair had a wave in front and a part on the side. He introduced himself as class president and he seemed so mature and composed for a seventeen-year-old.

His part of the program was to talk about "deportment." At first Ron didn't know what that word meant, and the boys sitting around him made rude noises and poked each other, already fidgety and bored with the whole thing. He told a story about a fictitious student named "Little Johnny," and how Little Johnny's been messing up. Little Johnny thinks he can get away with things, thinks rules don't apply to him. But he better watch out, because he'll get caught, and there will be consequences. He could even get kicked out of school. So no cutting classes, or leaving campus without a lunch pass, and we better not catch him smoking in the restrooms. Although it was all about school rules, everyone became captivated by the tale of Little Johnny. In the three or four minutes of the talk, Ron knew Stan was someone he could look up to and admire, but also someone he would never get to know.

Stan turned a page of his book, and while still reading pulled a cigarette from a pack of Lucky Strikes, lit it, and set the lighter down. Ron didn't think he would remember him, but he decided to introduce himself anyway.

"Stan? Stan Wilson?"

He looked up and there was a flicker of recognition in his eyes. "We were at Madison together, right? Cross country?"

"Yes," Ron said. "Cross country. That's right. I'm surprised you remember. You were a senior and I was a lowly sophomore."

"Well, it was a small team. And sort of a masochistic sport, don't you think?"

"That's for sure. I only did it to get out of regular P.E. Cross country in the fall, track in the spring."

"Sorry, but I don't recall your name."

"Oh, sorry. Ronnie Cooper, I mean Ron. Ron Cooper."

"Well, Ronnie, or Ron. . ." he took a quick drag, stubbed out the cigarette, and offered his hand, "how've you been?"

Ron pulled out a chair and sat across from him. "I never knew you came here after high school," he said. "I figured you for a big university, with scholarships and all that."

"I didn't come here. I went into the Navy."

"The Navy? Really? Why would you do that?"

Stan hesitated a few seconds. "To see the world?" He reached for another cigarette, tapped it on the side of a Zippo, and lit up.

"Let's just say it seemed like a good idea at the time." Another pause. "So now I'm a freshman, just like you."

"You know what?" Ron said, "I was just working on a letter to my English teacher, from last year, at our 'alma mater'. Would you mind looking at it? It's to go with a book I'm returning to him in the mail. I want to make sure it has no mistakes.

"Sure," Stan said. "Let me see it."

Ron opened his notebook, and Stan put out his cigarette and took the cap off a fountain pen. He watched as Stan carefully read the letter through, and as he went back to the start and began editing. He pursed his lips while concentrating, and worked as if Ron wasn't there. When finished, he passed the page to Ron and screwed the cap back on his pen.

Ron scanned the heavily marked-up draft. "What does 'N.B.' stand for?"

"Essentially, 'note well'." He tapped a spot on the draft with the blunt end of his pen. "This is a comma splice. It should be two sentences. Or you could use a semicolon."

Stan looked at his watch and began putting things in his briefcase, and Ron stood up.

"Well." he said. "Thanks for the corrections. I certainly got what I asked for."

It was just a chance meeting and Ron rarely saw him on campus again. But later on, when he got close enough to the legal drinking age, he started noticing Stan in beer bars in the evenings, at watering holes popular with the college crowd. They mostly were busy gathering spots, with tables and chairs and pool tables, but he always would be sitting on a stool alone at the bar. He dressed different, too, more neat and clean than the rest of the crowd: ironed short-sleeve shirts with button-down collars, khakis, and penny loafers. Some people suspicioned he was an off-duty cop, or a narc.

Ron started joining him for a glass or two. He became friendlier; as soon as Ron would sit down, he'd greet him with "What's your poison?" Then he'd signal the barkeep to bring his choice, and would wave off any attempt by Ron to pay for it.

They began spending more time together, talking, but always in bars. They had a mutual interest in American literature. Ron was enthused about Kerouac and Vonnegut; Stan was all about Hemingway and the post-War writers, like Jones, and Mailer. They critiqued novels they were reading and classes they were taking. Stan declared an English major and Ron wasn't sure yet—maybe psychology. They each were proud of their vocabularies and sometimes would spar over who knew the most abstruse words. But Stan never talked about being in the Navy or what happened those three years between high school and college. He lived alone and supported himself working as a night watchman for an amusement park. Ron still was living at home with his parents and avoiding the draft with student deferments.

Before long they graduated from beer bars to cocktail lounges, places where no one ordered bottled beer. Their favorite spot became a nice restaurant with a horseshoe-shaped bar. They'd sit in low, black leather swivel chairs, nursing Scotch in various concoctions. Later they might move to a booth for a midnight supper. Stan continued to look a little straight-arrow, with his short hair, V-neck sweaters and cordovan loafers. It was getting well into the Sixties, and long hair was the norm, but he always was neatly trimmed and clean-shaven. He never got interested in drugs, even a little grass, but he continued to be a steadfast drinker. One night, when it got to be closing time, they weren't ready to call it a night. Stan suggested going back to his place for coffee and maybe a nightcap.

He lived in an older part of town near the college, on a street lined with old pepper trees. His place was a small converted garage behind a Spanish-style stucco house. It was only a single garage to begin with, so a kitchenette, shower stall and toilet had been added on to the back. He plugged in a chrome percolator and made coffee while Ron looked around. The walls and ceiling had been finished with knotty-pine paneling, providing a comfortable cabin feel. Along one wall were built-in clothes drawers and shelves for books, and a small tightly-made bunk with a grey wool blanket. The opposite wall had the only window, a maple-trimmed couch with matching captain's chair, and a floor lamp in the corner.

They carried around their coffee cups—thick ceramic mugs—while Stan showed Ron various items. He had the usual collection of matchbooks in an oversized snifter, but his were from hotels and bars around the South Pacific. There was a dated portable record player with detachable speakers, but only a few LP's, mostly folk music. He pointed out several spoken word records by Beat poets. He had picked them up at the City Lights Bookstore in San Francisco. Also a collection of Zippo lighters, which he kept in a walnut silverware chest, in drawers lined with green felt. Some were still new in their snug boxes, but most were loose and well worn, with various inscriptions on them, or engravings of war ships plowing through waves.

156

After the tour, Stan asked him whether he wanted to stay longer, have a nightcap. When Ron agreed, he took a decanter of brandy from the bookcase, poured some into each of their cups, and settled into the captain's chair. He motioned for Ron to sit at the near end of the small couch. Then he lit a cigarette and just looked at him while the smoke collected under the shade of the floor lamp. He seemed to be deciding something and Ron waited, wondering what was coming. Then Stan got up and took what looked like a photo album from a drawer and sat with it in his lap.

"You know I was in the Navy," he said, "but I never told you what happened."

"Yeah, I was wondering about that."

He opened the cover and took out a newspaper clipping and several official-looking papers. Ron thought he was going to show him a commendation of some sort, or some pictures from his time in the Navy, but the mood had shifted to something heavy, ominous even.

"I haven't told anyone about this. I was recruited while in high school for a special program that could lead to becoming an officer. I went in two weeks after graduating from Madison and completed basic training at Camp Pendleton. I turned eighteen during basic."

For the first time since Ron had gotten to know him he looked unsure of himself, nothing like the confident senior class president, addressing the student body. Nor like the erudite English major, critiquing novels and showing off his editing ability. He was sitting stiffly on the edge of the chair and the clipping in his hand trembled slightly.

"I was in boot camp side-by-side with a bunch of gung-ho jarheads. I thought I was ready for anything, but there were times when I didn't think I was going to make it. Anyway, I got through that and was assigned to *USS Tioga*, docked down in San Diego. We were in port a few weeks for onboard training and drills, and then shipped out for Hawaii and the Philippines."

"So that would have been…late summer of '60."

"Right. You know how big an aircraft carrier is? It's a floating city. Three thousand, four hundred and forty-eight able-bodied seamen and officers. One hundred aircraft."

He sat back and considered Ron again, still looking unsure about something.

"I got drummed out because of a false accusation."

"What? 'Drummed out.' You mean, like, kicked out?"

He leaned forward in his chair. "I mean, *like*, held in the ship's brig for a month, restricted to quarters in San Diego, given a Section 8 discharge, and then marched off the base in broad daylight with other Navy wash-outs, miscreants, and fuck-ups."

Ron took a deep breath and let it out. "Jesus. What happened? Did you go AWOL or something?"

Stan gave a sardonic laugh and sat back. "I wish that's all it was. I was found in a berth with another sailor."

"In a berth. In a bed?"

"I was kicked out because the Navy thought I was a queer. I'm not."

Not knowing what to say, Ron waited for more. Stan stubbed out his cigarette and poured more brandy into their cups.

"We were in Pearl Harbor and it was our last shore leave before returning to San Diego. There was a group of us drinking and shooting pool and celebrating going home. I remember up to last call. We were all chanting 'last call for alcohol' and hammering shots, but nothing after that. Not how I got back to the ship or anything. Next thing I knew there was a flashlight in my face and two MP's were pulling me out of a strange bunk. I didn't know where I was, or what had happened."

"You mean the Navy kicked you out for *that*?"

He looked at Ron and his face was flushed and somehow showed a mixture of frustration, anger, and sadness all at the same time.

"You know what the worst part was? The way they did it. A Marine detail escorted us off the base and out to a bus stop on the main highway. There were about six of us that day, all in civvies. They marched us, in a tight little formation, out through the main gate and up the street, complete with the little 'hup hups'. They stopped traffic to make way for our detail, and we were marched down the middle of the fucking street to the bus stop. It makes the local news in San Diego, complete with names and the kind of discharge."

He looked at the papers in his lap. "'Stanford Alan Wilson, unfit for further service'."

He closed the album, dropped it to the floor and sank back in his chair, rubbing his eyes with the heels of his hands. Ron thought about the words "drummed out," and wondered if it meant being marched out to a drumbeat, just like Stan had described.

"Actually Ron, if you don't mind, I think I'll turn in. You can stay if you want—that couch folds out, but I need to hit the rack."

Ron didn't know what to do. He felt bad for him, but was at a total loss for words. He went to his car but just sat there, holding his keys in his lap, shivering. The clock in the dash showed 4:30. Stan's story kept replaying in his head, and he remembered how he had looked on the track that bright sunny morning in high school: senior class president, confident, on top of the world. Someone who already knew what he wanted to do with his life. Turned eighteen in the Navy. Happy birthday. Now it made sense why he was such a loner, a night watchman, why he drank so much.

After a while he went back up the driveway. A light still glowed behind the window shade. He stood on the porch a minute and then quietly knocked. Stan opened the door a few inches, and then let him back in.

He was in white boxer shorts and t-shirt and had been in bed. Neither of them said anything. He moved the coffee table out of the way and opened the couch into a small bed. It had sheets but no cover, and he got a blanket from a drawer. Ron took off his shoes and lay down. He thought Stan was going to put the blanket over him, but instead he turned off the floor lamp and lay down behind him and put his arm around him. He remembered his mother would sometimes take an afternoon nap with him, when he was very young, and she would call it "laying like spoons." After a minute Ron turned toward him, to say something, but Stan kissed him on the mouth. It felt natural, familiar even, like all the times he had kissed and made out with girls, going back to middle school, except for the soft sandpaper feel of stubble against his face and lips. They continued a while—embracing and kissing, and then Stan moved Ron on to his stomach and began to rub himself against his hip and ass. The kissing had felt unexpectedly natural, but it was turning into something else. Stan's breathing deepened and soon he unbuttoned and tugged down Ron's Levis. He went back to rubbing against him, and after a short time he pulled down Ron's underwear and tried to enter him.

He seemed to have difficulty penetrating, and as soon as he tried it was painful. Ron began to squirm and twist under him, but Stan only became more determined. The acidic bite of black coffee and brandy rose in his throat and he felt a wave of nausea.

"Wait, wait," he managed to say. "There's something wrong. It hurts."

Stan paused. "What? What's wrong?"

"It hurts too much. You'd better stop."

Instead he slid his hands under Ron's armpits, gripped his shoulders and resumed thrusting.

Ron couldn't tell if he was in or still trying to force his way, but after a long minute Stan did stop. Breathing heavily, he shifted his weight to one side and buried his face in the back of Ron's neck. All Ron had felt the whole time was a deep burning sensation, accompanied by Stan's raspy breathing in his ear. Then he rolled onto his back. Ron stayed on his stomach with his face turned away. He felt the cool night air on his backside.

Gray morning light was beginning to seep around the edges of the window shade. Stan got up and found his cigarettes, lit up, and then sat heavily on the side of his bunk. He sat hunched over, elbows on knees, staring at the floor. Ron pulled up his pants and went into the tiny john next to the kitchenette. There was no door, just a small American flag covering the top half of the opening. There was a sweet musty smell of mildew mixed with Old Spice aftershave. He sat on the toilet a while, relieved himself, and then carefully wiped to check for semen or blood.

He was sore to the touch. There didn't seem to be any of either, but he didn't want to turn on a light to make sure.

When he came out from the toilet Stan was laying back on his bed, feet still on the floor, mouth open, lightly snoring. The cigarette, now a drooping column of ash, was between two fingers by his side. He didn't want Stan to wake up, so he carefully removed it and put it out.

The next day was Sunday and he slept until early afternoon and then lay in bed thinking about the night before, and about the past few years hanging out with Stan. He wondered how he could have gotten everything so wrong, and whether he should have seen it coming. The same questions kept gnawing at him: Why did he go back? What was the kissing about? For that he had been more than acquiescent. And what if "it"—he was still getting used to the idea of having been fucked—had not been painful?

He decided he couldn't leave things the way they were, and so far Stan hadn't made any attempt to contact him. No "morning after" call. Late in the afternoon he drove to Stan's. He found the door ajar, and wondered if that meant he was expected. When he knocked, Stan said "It's open."

He was in his bunk propped up by a pillow, with the sheet neatly turned down a few inches over the blanket. There was an open book face down on the bed. The sofa bed had been returned to a sofa and everything was tidied up and back in place—no dirty cups or ashtrays, except the one on the floor by his bunk. No sign of the album or papers about his discharge. With the window open and blind up, and late afternoon sunlight streaming in, the small room was airy and looked larger than the dim, close night before. The small American flag covering the door to the toilet almost looked festive.

"You came back," Stan said, with a hint of a smile.

"Yeah but just to clarify a few things, about last night."

Stan patted the edge of his bed. "Sit down."

Ron hesitated, but sat.

"What happened last night—I'm not that way. I'm very straight—one hundred percent."

"You sure?" Stan said. "When you came back, I thought we were on the same page."

"I know I came back, but it wasn't for that."

"Why did you, then?"

"I really don't know. Naiveté, apparently."

"Can I do something?" Stan asked.

Before Ron could respond he reached into his lap and felt his crotch. "Okay," he said, laying back against his pillow, "I can tell you're not 'that way'."

Ron felt a stirring of revulsion and stood. "Well. I just wanted to clear the air. I'm taking off."

Stan reached down for his cigarettes on the floor.

Ron paused at the door. "You know, not only are we not on the 'same page,' we're not in the same world."

"That's too bad."

"And all that stuff about how you got kicked out of the Navy. Did that really happen?"

"All of it. Just like I said."

"But you said you're not a queer—that the Navy got it all wrong."

Stan looked away, toward the window. "I don't know what I am."

* * *

They knew some people in common, and over the next few years Stan occasionally would turn up, always alone, at birthday parties, graduations, and such. The last time Ron saw him was after he had married and started a family. He and his wife had organized a small cocktail hour fundraiser at their home. They were protesting a ballot measure that would stop "homosexuals" from becoming public school teachers. Stan came by, and when Ron was alone in the kitchen for a moment, he approached him.

"So this ballot initiative—I'm surprised you're so invested. What's that about?"

"It's about civil rights. Doesn't matter who's being discriminated against. I also backed the ACLU position on the Skokie march."

"Ah...," he said. "I see."

"You didn't come here just to support the cause, did you?"

Stan hesitated, but held Ron's eyes. "I was wondering if your apparent interest in gays could possibly extend to me."

"You know I'm married now, and have a baby. That should tell you something."

"Yes, of course. But you never know—know for sure, I mean."

164

REVELATION

Jonathan Everitt

And his arm lay around my breast—
And that night I was happy.

- Walt Whitman

And I was astonished.

    A stack of calendars, its dreams

    pressed dead and closet-dark.

How had this night come?

    How many years without the heft of

    another's arm to gird my breast?

How many cycles of moons and morning stars

    had left a lonely crater where

    this warm limb now came to rest

(as out our window all the lilacs breathed sweet their evening song

    unpressed, alive with their

    pink and blue blood)?

O the lifetime of grim hymns vibrating from within,
O the unrung telephones from numbers never given. Until

this pheromone bomb and eye

contact chemistry across

    a sticky hardwood bar.

Jukebox of bad music summoning

    a rush of lost gravity

    between two mouths until

morning: the weightlessness of a new world, welcome.

GIRL, YOU KNOW ITS TRUE COLORS

Allison L. Fradkin

CHARACTERS

*The women may be of any age and ethnicity and should vary
in their presentation and representation of femininity.*

Chick Van Dyke

Portia de Bossy

Jody Twatley

Pearl Gaily

The characters' names complement—and often complicate—their personalities.

SETTING

Home of Portia de Bossy.

TIME

A pleasant afternoon in the fall of 1989.

At rise, CHICK VAN DYKE is preparing products for a beauty demonstration party. The products come out of a shapely case that proudly displays the company name: Very Gay Cosmetics. Partygoer PORTIA DE BOSSY gets a load of the lipsticks. Her girlfriend, party pooper JODY TWATLEY, gets acquainted with a bottle of moisturizer.

JODY

Hello, friends. I'm your Vita-meata-*vaj*-amin Girl. Are you—

PORTIA

Jody Twatley, you put down that bittle lottle this instant! You mustn't be grody, Jody. That's Vita-meata-*veg*-amin.

(winks à la Lucy, then hands bottle back to Chick)

I apologize for my lady friend's uncouth behavior.

CHICK

Think nothing of it. I'm sure she's just a little nervous about today. Not all of us are comfortable with the idea of something other than vaj-amin sitting on our face. Are we, Ms. Twatley?

JODY

It makes me feel like I'm hiding. There's a reason they call it concealer. Conceal her? I'd rather look straight at her.

PORTIA

But you always look so gay, sweetheart. And I love it.

168

(Portia and Jody kiss.)

CHICK

You know what's even better than kissing, ladies? Kissing and making up. For that I recommend our Rubyfruit Jungle Red Lipstick—for the lezzie who likes the wet-lip look. Care to try some? Now, before you answer, be warned that it is very addictive. You'll be able to take the lipstick off the lesbian, but you won't be able to take the lesbian off the lipstick.

PORTIA

Let's get it on!

JODY

Just remember, dear: Anything you can do, I can do wetter.

PORTIA

I can do anything wetter than you.

JODY

No, you can't.

PORTIA

Yes, I—

CHICK

Can we break this up? Should you two do the same, we offer a
wonderful Ex Foliant. Breakups lead to breakouts, and a lady's skin
should always be as queer as possible. Do you agree, Ms. Bossy?

PORTIA

Yes, of course I agree—with the breakout, not the breakup. And it's *de*
Bossy, remember?

JODY

De Bossiest, and don't you forget it.

CHICK

Girls, please. We were supposed to begin ten minutes ago. Let's make
like Lizzie Borden and chop-chop, shall we?

JODY

You giving Pearl the ax there, lady?

PORTIA

Goodness, no!
              (to Chick)
We're expecting one more guest: our friend Pearl Gaily. As you know,
she tends toward tardiness.

JODY

She's our very special version of a late-in-life lesbian.

170

CHICK

I see. Well, when everyone's favorite dilatory dyke, Ms. Gaily, decides to make an appearance, then I will do my best to improve her appearance. Until then, I will work with what I have.

> (She gestures for Portia and Jody to take their seats. They do.)

All right, gals, are you ready?

> (Portia and Jody respond with differing degrees of delight. Chick recites the company mantra with alarming alacrity and some seriously scintillating choreography.)

We'll make you cream / for your face / Give you the brush / for your make-up case / If you're an L-A-D-Y...K-E / you'll look better / to the letter / You'll look spiffy / in a jiffy / Beyond eyeshadow of a doubt! / Gayvon calling!

> (Portia and Jody respond appropriately—or not.)

Hello, and welcome to a Very Gay product demonstration party. I'm Chick Van Dyke, decorated beauty consultant with the company. Now, why have you gals called me here this afternoon? Because ever since the passage of the Silly Lezbetter Fair Pay Act—not to be confused with the Lilly Ledbetter Fair Pay Act, which won't be signed on the dotted line for another twenty years—the wage gap between the fair sex—Sapphics, specifically—and the opposite sex—that is to say, male homosexuals— has closed...not completely but, considerately, considerably. As a result, we are no longer approaching another Gay Nineties. We're gearing up for a Lesbian Nineties! More importantly, you and you and I will have more disposable income to spend on such necessities as: women, theatre tickets for when we'd like to experience a different kind of dyke drama

CHICK (c'td)

than we normally do with women, and make-up—to get the attention of women.

JODY

But if straight women use make-up to attract the opposite sex, shouldn't we do the opposite to attract the same sex? We are different, after all.

CHICK

Just because we're different, Ms. Twatley, doesn't mean we aren't the same. Furthermore, women beautify. It's tradition. And because the Lezbetter legislation is still pretty recent, we have a lot of making up to do!

PORTIA

Does it only help lesbians? I mean, I am a lesbian, so I never gave it much thought since it doesn't affect me; it benefits me. But Lezbetter? The name alone suggests that—

CHICK

What's in a name?

JODY

You tell us, Chick Van Dyke. Not all letters are created equal, you know. That's why we needed this legislation—because everyone always put the G before the L. And that doesn't suit all of us to a T.

CHICK

Inclusivity is implied. In theory, the law benefits all individuals who identify as women and who have survived any and all attempts at the heterosexualization of women. But if you insist on shaking things up, then I insist on making things up.

JODY

What is this? A reboot of *The Lucy-Lezzie Comedy Hour*?

PORTIA

Will you please stop picking on her?

JODY

You were picking on her.

PORTIA

I was picking her brain.

CHICK

And I am picking a volunteer. Ms. Twatley, you'll come join me, won't you?

JODY

(joylessly joining her)

Are you going to make me into a paragon of femininity?

CHICK

A paragon? Try an octagon. Let the application process begin! When I get through with you, my dear, you are going to feel like a natural woman. Anyone who's ever made you feel otherwise will see the error of their ways when they see you wearing our waterproof mascara: Lashing Out. In fact, it might even cause a few eyes to *wand*-er...right down to your lips, because who could gloss over our latest lip gloss, Boi – with an "i" – senberry Jam?

JODY

Don't you have anything a little more...unvarnished?

CHICK

Ms. Twatley, please. It's not as if the "i" in "boi" is dotted with a heart, for heaven's sake. There's no need to worry that it will "varnish" your reputation. Or ours. Because it's made with real boysenberries – the original spelling, of course – among other things.

JODY

Like what?

PORTIA

Pride.

CHICK

You've been reading our labels, haven't you?

PORTIA

Labels are not just for lesbians.

CHICK

Right you are, Ms. de Bossy. You see, we at Very Gay not only take pride in our products; we put pride in them. So when you wear our make-up, your inner beauty comes out. Look at how beautiful Ms. Twatley is inside.

JODY

(scrutinizes her reflection in Chick's hand mirror)
You are indeed a mirror-cle worker, Ms. Van Dyke.

CHICK

Thank you very gay. Much! Gay much? Naturally! So am I. Well, thank you, Jody, very much, for putting your face in my hands. We have a saying in the beauty business: Make like a compact and click! And that's just what we did, didn't we?

JODY

I've got chills – they're beautifying! Sell me more, sell me more.

PORTIA

(to Chick)
How much dough did she spend?

PORTIA (c'td)

(to Jody)

Oh, no matter. Anything you can buy, I can buy cheaper.

JODY

I can buy anything cheaper than you.

CHICK

No, you can't. The prices are fixed. But remember, friends, you needn't be frugal any longer. Silly Lezbetter? Hello! You're sitting pretty now, which means you can sit even prettier – and pricier! Embrace your financial lesbiandependence, ladies!

PORTIA

Show me how to apply the lip gloss?

CHICK

Certainly. First, twist the cap until it is openly gay—

(PEARL GAILY enters, though not very gaily.)

PEARL

Don't let her demonstrate on you! That's what she does. She demon*straights* on innocent lesbians!

CHICK

Ms. Gaily! At long last. You remember me: Chick Van Dyke.

(Chick attempts to cross to Pearl for a handshake and takes a Dick Van Dyke-like pratfall in the process.)

JODY

Ah-ah-ah. Chick before Dick.

(Pearl bursts into tears.)

PORTIA

My word, Pearl, what on earth has got you carrying on like the Princess of Wails?

PEARL

That glamour scammer, that's what! She knowingly sold me products that were defective. Remember that Rubyfruit Jungle Red Lipstick, Ms. Van Dyke?

CHICK

I remember it looked marvelous on your mouth.

PEARL

Don't try to kiss up to me, you Rita Mae Brown-noser. I'll bet that batch contained phalluses!

CHICK

Those, Ms. Gaily, are not on our list of approved ingredients. And I believe you mean phthalates, although the P is silent.

PEARL

Yeah, well, thanks to you, so is the L! And now the only way to keep these waterworks at bay is with a dike.

PORTIA

Will I do?

        (hands her handkerchief to Pearl, who makes good use
        of it)

Better?

        (at Pearl's indication of appreciation)

Good. But it's best if you tell us what the trouble is, Pearl, so we can help you.

PEARL

I can keep a straight face, that's what the trouble is. Look at it. Pretty soon I'll lose all my lovely laugh lines and have no redeeming features. I've already lost my lesbian tendencies, and don't know where to find them. I thought the search would be over once I stopped using the Very Gay stuff, but no such luck. Exactly one month ago today, when I attended my first beauty consultation party, I made up my mind to make up my face with these products and now I'm facing the consequences. Now I'm struggling with…with…with opposite-sex attraction.

PORTIA

(embracing Pearl)

My, my. Now, now. Let's not k.d. languish in despair.

JODY

Quit your Pearl-clutching, would you? A fellow gal's dykedom has disappeared and it's up to us to figure out where it went.

PORTIA

I'm so glad Emma Chemical Peel is on the case.

JODY

Actually, dear, I prefer Harriet the Spry, because I'm gonna bust that case wide open!

(Jody advances on Chick's make-up case. Chick throws herself in front of it in a supremely sacrificial fashion.)

CHICK

It isn't in there!

PORTIA

Perhaps you were experiencing a bout of internalized lesbophobia and checked it at the closet door?

PEARL

No. No, I don't think so. Phooey, pooh, and harrumph. I can't believe this is happening again!

> (singing, to the tune of "Where Has My Little Dog Gone?")

Oh where oh where has my Sapphic self gone? Oh where oh where can it be?

PORTIA

> (singing)

With her queer cohort—

CHICK

> (singing as she's stifling Pearl's sobs)

—and her wail cut short—

PORTIA and JODY

> (singing)

Oh where oh where can it be?

CHICK

I've got it!

PEARL

I knew it!

CHICK

No. "Where can it be?" B! That's the letter you're looking for. You see, Ms. Gaily, by admitting it's happening again, you're acknowledging it's happened before, thereby confessing it's—you're—bisexual.

(Silence. Pearl and her pals proceed to process this.)

PEARL

Gee whiz, are you saying that the only part of me that's lesbian is the b-i in the middle?

CHICK

You are but a blip and a pip on my very gaydar. Therefore, even if you discontinued the usage of our products within hours of your first application, our make-up cannot change your…makeup. Our products are simply not formulated to produce, induce, or reduce one's lesbianism. And no matter how often you used our hydrating face mist, it would have been impossible for you to spray away the gay.

PEARL

I guess not. I suppose that…bisexual…is a logical label. But…I mean…Well, what's expected of me? What are the bi-laws? Does that Lezbetter Act still apply to me?

PORTIA

Absolutely. It stipulates only that you be lady-liking. It does not specify percentages.

PEARL

Okay, that's one lez thing—sorry, one fewer thing—to worry about. What else? Do I come out of a closet or just a drawer? I can still be part of your world, can't I?

PORTIA and JODY

(à la *Annie Get Your Gun* again)

Yes, you can. Yes, you can!

PEARL

Good, great. Phew! Gosh, I wish I could see myself. Not my own image, but a replica – a representation, you know? It would make me feel so much…more real. Perhaps on that new show *Family Matters*. Its theme song is "As Gays Go Bi."

PORTIA

Days, dear. As in: One of these days, you will see yourself. In the meantime, you're still one of the family, Pearl, and that's all that matters.

CHICK

Well, aren't you the picture of parity. Her last name is Gaily. You don't think she should live up to it?

JODY

She will live up to it—when she accepts herself.

PORTIA

That's right—because you spell Gaily with an "i." Know what else you spell with an "i"?

PEARL

Bi?

PORTIA

Exactly! And you dot the "i" with a big old heart.

CHICK
(packing up her cosmetics)
FYI, Ms. Gaily, you can credit—and even thank—Very Gay Cosmetics for our role in the discovery of your bisexuality, but you cannot blame us for causing it. In addition, I must inform you that our make-up does not cover pre-existing conditions.

JODY

Lighten up, lady.

CHICK

Our make-up does not do *that* either. A woman's complexion is a complex thing, not a thing that should give a woman a complex.

JODY

The same goes for her sexuality, even if it is not exclusively same-sex oriented. Or is lesbianism a form of discrimination?

CHICK

Of course not! But the company is called Very Gay for a reason.

JODY

Beauty school cop-out. We have a saying *for* the beauty business: Make like a looking glass and reflect. Because sometimes, saying "gay" is no different than saying "guys" when you really mean "girls" or mixed company. Inclusivity is implied.

PEARL

You said it!

CHICK

No, I said it. And I'm—she's—right.

PEARL

So I can keep using your products?

PEARL

Oh, please, Ms. Van Dyke. Make me up before you go-go!

(Chick vacillates, hesitates, capitulates.)

CHICK

My job is to help you not only realize but dramatize the phenomenal woman you are on the inside. Even if that phenomenal woman happens

184

CHICK (c'td)

to be less of a lesbian than I am, I suppose it doesn't mean that she's less than I am.

PEARL

In that case, let's see if there's something good in *that* case.

JODY

(unpacking the cosmetics case)

Just remember, Pearl: The answer to all your problems is not in any of these bittle lottles – or little bottles, or tubes, or compacts. Because you, pal o' mine, do not have any problems. Not where any of this sexuality stuff is concerned, anyway.

PEARL

Thank you, Jody, and thank you, Pearl, and thank you, Ms. Van Dyke, for *B*-ing a friend.

JODY

Hey, Ms. V.D., what do you say we do that company mantra, cutesy cheer thing you did earlier? Pearl missed it.

CHICK

All right. Gals, are you ready? I require the utmost readiness.

PORTIA

We have more readiness than you can shake a lipstick at!

CHICK, JODY, and PORTIA

We'll make you cream / for your face / Give you the brush / for your make-up case / If you are L, G, B, T, or Q / you'll look better / to the letter / You'll look spiffy / in a jiffy / Beyond eyeshadow of a doubt! / Gayvon calling!

> (Pearl participates in a repetition of the recitation, and Chick has a gay old time complicating the choreography. The others attempt to follow her but can't. Each eventually ends up doing her own thing.)

CHICK

Now, now, ladies. This is "The Chick Van Dyke Show." It's my way—

PEARL, JODY, and PORTIA

—or the bi way!

CHICK

Precisely. Because this make-up maven is no longer an up-stander. She's a bi-stander!

PEARL

And that, like your lipstick, is totally tubular.

> <u>Curtain.</u>

186

FOSSIL FUELED

Aimee Herman

Everyone else rubbed UV protectant onto skin,
flirted shoulders with oncoming traffic and the wind

while he walked to Prospect Park with suicide
note and kerosene, giving himself back to the earth.

There are days I think about setting my scars on fire
to see what shape I might melt into.

There are days I grow numb trying to understand how
far down the trees' roots go or why letters in an alphabet

like LGBTQ make people so angry. Just yesterday, I breathed in
eight million skin cells and the secret messages of squirrels.

Everyone seems to be on a diet of hate these days; I just want
to get through a day where tongues tie us into love letters not

tombstones.

PIECING TOGETHER A FRACTURED LIFE: A COMING OUT STORY

Robert Kenneth Anderson

1.

A Leap, a Look Back

I came out in my late thirties, in 1980, after sixteen years of marriage. Totally closeted my whole life till then, when I was finally ready to take that leap into the unknown, I came out like gangbusters. I'd tell anyone who would listen, even strangers at the bus stop. I'd tell friends I hadn't seen in years, often in casual conversation or over the phone. "Oh, there's something you should know…" I could squeeze the information into almost any situation, like a 60-second public service announcement. I spared only the aged and infirm: my 96-year-old grandfather who had just entered a nursing home, and my 80-year-old great aunt who was dying from emphysema. I'm surprised I showed that much restraint.

Coming out was an eruption of expressive freedom for me. A secret so horrible I could barely admit it to myself, much less anyone else, was out in the open at last. Within a few weeks of deciding to come out, I had told my wife, my ten-year-old daughter, my parents, all my friends, my colleagues at work. I didn't even care if my supervisor found out. It wasn't exactly a decision any longer; I simply *had* to tell. The pressure from a lifetime of shame and secrecy had built to the bursting point.

When I came out, almost forty years ago now, a friend from work who was a cartoonist, gave me a card she had designed based on her own experience of being married and coming out as a lesbian. On the cover is a closet door open just a crack, with two eyes near the floor peering anxiously out of the darkness. On the inside, the door is flung wide open and the figure has sprung out into the light, head thrown back, hair standing on end with excitement, arms flung open to the world in ecstasy, propelled into the future as if through the uncoiling of a giant spring. That gesture says it all.

To get the energy here, some history helps. In the Forties and Fifties when I grew up, the very topic of homosexuality, the word itself, was taboo. If handled at all in books and movies, the subject was treated obliquely, through hint and innuendo, and always with dire consequences for the offender... though exactly what the offense was, you were never really sure. The "love that dare not speak its name" was beyond the pale, relegated to the shadowy netherworld of sin and vice, shrouded in shame and guilt. Police raided gay bars and bathhouses, men were jailed for having sex with other men, suspected homosexuals were purged from public office.

I came of age in the homogenized, sanitized Fifties when it sometimes seemed that Sex itself was taboo. Married couples were shown sleeping in separate beds in movies and TV, and a couple having sex might be insinuated through a pair of pumps overturned at bedside while fireworks erupted in the night sky. These were the postwar boom years when most middle-class families were still intact and society was knit together by broadly shared values and norms, with everything reinforced in the popular media through uplifting narratives and glossy,

190

idealized images. It was a great time to grow up, if you fit those norms, but woe betide the boy who didn't. Perhaps sensing deep down that I was different, without a clue what that meant, I played it safe, strictly by the rules, and took the mores of that conformist culture too much to heart. I blush to say, that unlike my gay brothers who rebelled and dared to be different, whatever the costs, I bought the script whole-cloth. My favorite TV show at the time was *Father Knows Best*; my favorite artist, Norman Rockwell. "The best little boy in the world"—that was my cover, and when the lid came off, it blew!

Looking back, I'm not particularly proud of how I came out. The initial energy was driven, ferocious. While the sex was never anonymous or compulsive, it was casual and recreational, often careless of others' feelings. In telling people I was gay, I slighted their need to receive the information in a way that would help them deal with it. I told my young daughter at the same time she learned that her mom and I were divorcing, before tucking her into bed one night. Rachel knew we'd been in couples counseling and cried at the news of the divorce, then laughed when I explained that I was gay. She quickly reached out to touch my arm.

"I'm sorry, Dad, it just sounds funny—it's so *weird*." Then came the inevitable question: "What do two men do, anyway?" Like too many kids these days, Rachel was precocious, grown-up beyond her years…and more brave than any kid should have to be.

I'm least proud of how I told her; I put little thought into what to say or when and how to say it. I know men who have agonized over these questions. One friend discussed with a support group for a year the decision of when to tell his teenage son, then decided to wait till the

191

boy was safely through adolescence. His younger son, who was homophobic, he chose not to tell until his late twenties, putting the older son in an awkward bind. These questions of timing are always dicey and can be answered in many different ways. Let the record show, I didn't hesitate, not for a minute.

I rationalized: I've dealt with this problem my entire life, carried the full weight of it by myself. It's taken its toll in paralysis and depression. Let others deal with it for a change… and I let go, as simple as that. I let go of a lifetime of deceiving myself and others, of denying and compartmentalizing my feelings, of pretending and playing roles and being phony with the people I loved most. I had lived a lie—no more!

Behind my impulsiveness and insensitivity, perhaps in some sense redeeming them, lay a newfound *joie de vivre*, an openness to life and all it has to teach, a hunger for the truth and a desire to be made whole.

I want to say, after I came out, I never looked back, and in one sense that's true. I have met this experience with open arms. I have no regrets about this odyssey of discovery. It has proved a source of renewal and energy that infuses itself to this day into nearly every corner of my life. MY capacity for friendship and love, my willingness to embark on new adventures, to push limits and test myself, my creativity and spirituality, all still take their energy from here, this radical declaration of freedom and independence.

It isn't that I don't have problems any more. I'm aging, I'm going blind, I still struggle with issues of intimacy, empathy, social responsibility, pride, wrath, sloth, lust, the whole panoply of human ills. The difference is, I own these problems, because I own my life. I am not playing out a role according to somebody else's rules and expectations; I am not watching my life unfold around me as if it belonged to somebody else. I choose, I act, I take responsibility, I grow. The struggle has meaning because it is mine.

A friend once said that being married and being gay, for him, was like living inside a glass jar. You saw everything that was happening to you, you went through the motions, but you didn't connect, you weren't fully present. You viewed yourself like a specimen under glass.

One man I knew could not speak of his marriage without weeping. Earl had been married for thirty-five years and was totally faithful to his wife. He loved her and was a dutiful, caring husband and father. She developed cancer and Earl took early retirement to nurse her through the last two years of her life. When she died, he came out at age 65— hardly prime time to put yourself on the market. Everywhere you went in the gay community—the bars, salons, parties, pot-lucks, card games— there was Earl, intense, lonely, garrulous, usually telling his story to some luckless guy who looked vaguely uneasy, like the wedding guest fingered by the glittery-eyed Ancient Mariner. Loneliness is hardly a strong selling point. Luckily Earl eventually found and fell in love with a younger guy and they moved to San Diego to set up housekeeping.

Throughout his marriage Earl had behaved honorably, with no reason to reproach himself. Yet on at least two occasions in a support group for married gay men we belonged to, I saw him break down when speaking of his wife and his marriage.

"I was false to her," he said through tears. "She never knew me for who I really was. I wasn't true, I always kept a part of myself hidden from her. She must have known, and it must have hurt her." His grief was inconsolable.

The grief of inauthenticity is a grief many married gay men share. It runs deep and takes many forms. Whether the issue is being true to yourself or another, betraying your own values or someone else's trust, or sacrificing an essential part of your sexuality or identity, the grief is immeasurable, because it goes to the core of your being. It's a painful predicament, yet I've never met a gay father who wasn't profoundly grateful for the opportunity to have children and raise a family. In those days, that meant getting hitched… the old-fashioned way.

We had a saying in the gay fathers support group where I met Earl and some of the other men whose stories figure in my writing: "You've got your chronological age, and then you've got your gay age, your real age, which dates from when you came out." The deep truth behind this statement is the transformative power of living authentically, but it was often said half-jokingly, to excuse adolescent behavior in otherwise mature, responsible adults. Group members were professionals in their late-thirties to mid-fifties, all committed family men who'd fallen deeply in love with a woman and managed to make the best of it till middle age forced a reckoning with their same-sex attraction.

At that point, coming out could definitely have its wild side. We sometimes called this the "candy-store phase"—"I'll take one of those and one of those, and that bright red one over there, and some of that gunky-looking stuff on the back shelf." It's funny, but sad too, for there's no way to make up for lost time, no way to recover an adolescence you never had.

When I came out, it was a full, joyous leap into an unknown future. Yet, like Earl and so many other gay married men, I'm haunted. I'm haunted by a marriage that failed, in part, because I passed through it in a daze of denial. I'm haunted by the hurt caused to three people—me, my ex-wife and my daughter—because I was trying so hard to be something I was not, and never could be. I'm haunted by the part of my life I never lived... by the boy I never knew.

The grief of the unlived life—many of us deal with it in one form or another, at some point in our lives. For me as a married gay man who came out later in life, it has a special poignancy, an existential edge. In some sense, it defines me.

2.

Boys I Never Knew

I moved through adolescence numb. I shut down my tender and erotic feelings because everything in my culture, spoken and unspoken, during the mid-Fifties when I came of age, told me they were unthinkable, unforgivable. To survive that tumultuous passage into adulthood, I learned to compartmentalize, to exist on two tracks simultaneously. With one part of my being, I kind of knew the truth about myself, while with the other, more dominant part, I fought and denied it with everything I had. Knowing and denying were like breathing in and breathing out.

* * *

I can retrace my adolescence as a series of lost moments. I remember the time in ninth grade when my best buddy, Arizona, said as we were lying on his bed, looking out the window and ogling two girls across the street who were enjoying the unaccustomed warmth of an early spring day in Minnesota: "You know, two boys could have a lot of fun too."

Arizona was a superb athlete, a handsome boy with jet-black hair, a hint of Native American in his features, one of those natural heroes with an easy grace who drew almost everyone to him. I looked at him, lying just two feet from me, with total incomprehension. What did those words mean? Surely he couldn't be saying them to me. I checked out; the words didn't register.

Not then, they didn't, but I have thought of them often since.

And I am left wondering, was it then that I stopped going over to his house almost every day after school? That was our routine. The thought only occurs to me forty-five years later. Arizona and I were very close. We went through confirmation together. The walls of his room were plastered with dozens of zany cartoons in the style of *Mad Magazine* that I had drawn just for him; he was the friend to whom I had confided my fears that I was jerking off too much. But at some point—I don't know when or why—I simply stopped seeing him. It's one of those curious gaps in my history.

Another occurred with a friend in eleventh grade. I was walking home from downtown Robbinsdale with Denny Nelson, who was going on and on about this girl he was seeing, how wonderful she was and how great it made him feel to have a steady girl.

"I hope you get a girl-friend, Bob. There's nothing like it, nothing like the love of a girl. It makes you feel good about yourself, that you're a man and you care about each other more than anything else in the world."

By this time, almost all the boys I hung out with were talking about girls. I had no interest. One girl was trying to date me, but this only made me vaguely uncomfortable, like something was expected of me. What? —I hadn't a clue. I had an almost determined innocence on the subject. But I liked it when boys talked about girls, even if I felt a little left out. It meant I was accepted, at least as an adjunct member, into the sacred fraternity of boys. I belonged. And it made me feel close to them because they opened up, made themselves vulnerable, in ways not typical between boys.

Denny was usually shy and quiet, but not this afternoon. When we got back to my house, we went into my brother's and my bedroom, closed the door and continued our conversation. He stretched out his lanky frame on my brother's lower bunk, which was U.S. Army surplus and sagged under his weight like a hammock. He clasped his hands behind his head and turned his face toward me to speak.

That's the last memory I have of the experience.

I like to imagine his long, thin face, with its well-defined contours, its ridges of brow and cheekbone, the crooked bridge of his nose broken in a fight, looking sensitive and softened in the muted light of late afternoon. What other words we said to each other, what I felt and what I thought afterwards, I don't recall. But the record is clear: I stopped seeing him after that, except for occasional pleasantries at school.

Why? Did I feel stirrings of a forbidden tenderness... attraction, desire? Everything else about the experience is vivid and etched into memory: the walk home, the conversation about girl-friends—it occurred as we crossed the railroad tracks and passed Triangle Park—the scene of Denny lying on the bed, the quality of light in the room.

Then memory stops, because feeling stops.

The sense of closeness, comforting during the walk home, becomes threatening. I do what I need to do to protect myself, without even knowing what I am protecting myself against. I disconnect; I terminate the friendship.

The only recollection of feeling I have from that conversation in the bedroom lingers to this day like the remnant of a nearly forgotten dream—something intense and vague that nags at the edge of consciousness, and disturbs the day's composure.

But it preserved the memory. Both of these experiences—with Arizona and Denny—while lost to me in certain respects, remain locked into memory, charged with a powerful yet indecipherable emotion. The key to unlocking the fullness of those moments, making sense of my history and recovering the boy I never had a chance to be, I receive only in adulthood, when I am ready to come out and accept myself as a gay man.

How many friendships with boys, and then later with men, followed this pattern of unaccountable termination? How many were short-circuited from ever developing in the first place?

A string of boys passed through my teenage years, appearing mostly in cameo roles, in brief, chance encounters that were much safer to manage than full friendships, and whose main purpose was to feed a starved imagination.

I remember Jerry, a cute, slight, blond go-fer at a resort on Lake Vermillion where my family vacationed the summer after ninth grade. I couldn't wait to finish breakfast every morning so I could hang out with him in the garage as he tinkered with boat motors and told funny stories about resort residents. I visited every chance I got during the day, and always felt a sinking feeling when I didn't find him there, bent over his workbench. I was jealous of his attentions to the other residents, and felt uneasy when he invited me to go riding with him and his buddies as they picked up girls in the nearby town of Tower. All I wanted was to be near him.

One morning he told me, with a sly wink and grin, about Jimmy, who had stuck his finger up a girl, then passed it around for the other guys in the car to smell. "Boy, did it stink!," he said, chuckling. Goody-two-shoes that I was, I thought this was crude and disrespectful to the girl, and wondered why she would let anyone do this to her.

Jerry seemed the master of everything he touched: motors, broken fishing reels, the pike and pan fish he gutted and scaled for the residents, and I suppose, even girls. I was in seventh heaven when he wanted to learn something I knew—how to do Art Deco lettering, something I had learned from an old sign-painting book my grandpa had given to me.

In that intense, too-short week, Jerry-charmed, I learned everything I could about him, his habits, thoughts, history, likes and dislikes. His life was mythical, every fact of it enchanted. I learned he liked quick-draw target shooting and that became the most fascinating topic in the world. Before my family left for home, I asked my dad to take me into Tower to a gun shop where I could buy Jerry a quick-draw holster. I included a note with the extravagant gift, which I laid reverentially at the shrine of his unattended workbench the morning we left, inviting him to visit me sometime in Robbinsdale. For at least two summers after that, I wondered dreamily if he would show up.

All of these activities—the fascination and obsession, the disappointment and jealousy, the gift and longing—grew bit by bit, a great sacred edifice encrusted around a mysterious, hollow core of something I couldn't name or acknowledge. I was an acolyte performing the meaningless rituals of a forgotten religion.

Two years after Jerry came Jack, the son of one of my dad's best friends, who paid a brief visit with his father one grey fall afternoon on a day-trip down from Duluth. We played catch with a football in the leaf-swept street in front of my house, running crazily after passes and punts skewed by the skittish wind. We ended the game hot and sweaty, exhausted and laughing. Jack suggested a quick shower together. Together? He was husky, ruddy and affable, more developed than I was and obviously more comfortable being naked in the company of other boys. I barely looked at him as we undressed in the tiny bathroom and stepped into the shower, and I kept my back to him, careful not to brush against him in the cramped quarters. By this time, I was skilled at self-containment—lots of practice turning to the wall and hunching over to undress in boys' locker-rooms, studiously averting my eyes and shutting out the sounds of their teasing and laughter.

For years after Jack's visit, however, I was much less reserved in fantasy, though never reckless. I revisited the scene again and again to bask in boyish affection. I had my fill of his frank good looks, his playful good nature; without shame I watched him undress, soap himself up and towel off in the safety zone of my imagination. Free of sex, these fantasies, countless scenarios salvaged from my few scraps of memory—whatever I had allowed myself to experience at the time—were about something unnamable, vague and idealized, and always tinged with yearning and regret. What had I missed?

My teenage years were dotted with such encounters, though they grew fewer as I grew older. I lived increasingly on the memory of a select few, which sustained me through an increasingly lonely adolescence.

Chief among these encounters—the most powerful, the one I returned to most often—was the boy I met one summer when I was sixteen on a family camping trip to Lake Itasca. I came upon him sitting by himself on a grassy knoll in a clearing at the edge of the lake. I can't retrieve the actual memory any longer. It is too embellished and shop-worn with use, shrouded in layers of association.

All that remains is a picture, a feeling. He is hunched forward, his elbows resting cavalierly on his knees, gazing across the water, his profile stark against its shimmering surface and cocked attentively to the far shore, a stem of grass pinched between his lips. In silhouette, he is reduced to a few clean strokes, all angles, poised, a calligraph: the grace of energy in repose.

I meet him as I break out of the brush after straying off the path through the woods. Did the suddenness of the encounter disarm us, create an instant rapport? Camaraderie—that's the core feeling. We had a brief conversation, that was all. I quickly forgot the content, the particulars. They weren't important. What mattered was memory. He became a cipher. With no name, no history, no face, he stood for any boy with whom I could feel close, and therefore, no boy. He was a screen onto which I could project anything I wanted, a trigger that released a flood of emotion. In countless returns to the scene, each one elaborated with minute variations, I drew whatever comfort I could from the core feelings of openness and closeness, which were magnified in imagination into a dream of impossible tenderness. Did we go for a swim, a walk in the woods, did we talk about our boyhood, our dreams and plans for the future? In conversation after conversation, that dream of closeness was refracted again and again, held up to the light of a wholly imaginary life.

The incident became hallowed, part of the lore of my growing up. It sustained me through my later adolescence and the early years of my marriage.

Thin gruel, I think now. And underneath nagged darker feelings: an impossible perfectionism, a bitter disappointment with life and a sense of personal failure and cowardice. I could not seize the moment. Could I even love? But what would I seize, and what would I love? And what really happened in that clearing? Anything? All this fretting and yearning and grieving were about something that never happened, never could happen, because I would not admit to myself what was going on.

By the time of my late teens and early twenties, therefore, I was profoundly lonely—"bone-lonely," I called it. Because I had no interest in girls, and because boys were strictly off-limits, I felt paralyzed, and I saw this paralysis as an inability to love, a deep moral flaw at the core of my being that set me apart from the rest of humanity.

3.

Gary at Poolside

You're a bolt of pink neon, jagged in tremulous blue. You dive deep with scissored kicks, skim the gritty bottom of the pool with your pug nose, shimmy along its Jell-O geometry, then twist and roll in rapid ascent. You shatter the shimmering film between us, leaving a pearly cream of bubbles in your wake. Dazzling efflorescence! You arch your back, loll lazily on the rippling surface and bare your smooth belly to my gaze. Your navel glistens, a tufted path points to jewels bobbing in the cleft of your groin.

None of this I saw then, not as I watched guardedly from pool's edge, watched the watcher watching. It was a studied scene: two boys swimming naked at the Y. I was relieved we were the only ones, relieved I watched without desire. It was like looking at snapshots taken with my Brownie Hawkeye: Gary at poolside, Gary poised on diving board, Gary blurred in mid-air and holding his nose while doing the cannonball. Each shot separate, contained, composed, in muted shades of grey, all of them slightly out of focus, and every one taken from too far away.

But months later I watched again, this time in sweet, shameful secrecy, watched as my family drove through the Badlands of South Dakota. I studied those shots again and again, up close and from every angle, tried to charge them with the vivid life I'd missed before. Not quite you, Gary, none of that boyish exuberance poised just this side of manly grace, none of that holy fire.

But enough… enough to stir me as I sat hot and cramped between my younger brother and maiden Aunt Augusta in the back seat of our '53 Studebaker.

Now, I watch again, reclaim in imagining what was nearly lost to memory. Shame streams from me like bubbles from a swimmer breaking for the surface, and you flash before me, more vivid and electric with each bold stroke.

* * *

At the time we went swimming, Gary was legendary in the neighborhood. He was rumored to be big—boys kept careful track of these things. The subject came up over Pepsis and baseball cards as I sat outside the corner grocery store with the Swanson kids and their new friend Franko, a tall, thin kid who wore sweatshirts even on the hottest summer days to hide his skinny arms.

"Gary's huge," one of them said.

"Bigger than Oberg?"

"You bet."

"You gotta be kidding. How do you know? You seen it?"

"Naw, but everybody who's seen it says so."

"Nobody's bigger than Oberg."

Let them talk, I thought, I'll soon see for myself. Gary had pestered me for months to go swimming at the downtown YMCA where, in those days, men and boys swam in the nude. I was reluctant—I was as skinny as Franko and slow to develop—but I had finally relented, and we were set to go. When the day arrived and I had steeled myself for the ordeal, it was as if secret emissaries from the Vatican had been dispatched to sanitize the scene. The offending genitalia had, in effect, been airbrushed out. Call it a supreme act of will, a triumph of my eternal vigilance. I saw nothing, or I remembered nothing, or what I saw was so nondescript, so eviscerated of life, it counted for nothing.

* * *

What I learned as a defense mechanism in adolescence—turning myself off to a present experience and recovering it later, at a safe remove, where its potency was diluted with longing and disappointment, and I could manage it within the strictures of conscious intention—became a reflex, an escape in early adulthood.

Now, in the fullness of middle age, retrospection has become a means of healing.

In coming out, I reclaim myself and my history. In remembering the boy Gary or any of the boys who passed through my adolescence, I remember the boy Robert, and in paying attention to unaccountable gaps in my history, to my anger, bitterness or any emotion that takes its charge from deeper wellsprings, I honor the loss and self-betrayal that boy endured.

And I move beyond them.

Remembering is a holy and healing act. For me the word means precisely that: a "re-membering," a piecing together of a fractured life, making it whole. *whole, holy, healing; Remembering, re-membering*—words have curious associations. In reference to Gary, "re-membering" takes on another dimension of meaning entirely.

In coming out, with that act of radical self-acceptance, I begin to make sense of my story. A curious synergy happens: the more integrated and actualized I become, the more freely memory flows for me, as if lending a hand in the process of healing. This is active, shaping memory, more than chance recollection or idle reminiscence. It is memory telling me what my life is about, where I have been and where I am going. It sifts and reorganizes, directs my attention, points out and fills in the gaps, making vital connections. It is revelatory, dynamic and organic, an energy that breathes through the raw materials of my life, showing me its pattern, telling me its story.

Note: This piece is adapted from parts of my self-published memoir, *Out of Denial: Piecing Together a Fractured Life* (Lulu.com, 2008).

MAXINE WHO WAS ONCE MAX

Stephen Scott Whitaker

O hormone, O
facial cream, dream
after dream after dream.
For her it is fingernail, warm belly,

shaping with corset
what nature has given her
into beauty, rather than the casket lines
she was born into; for the whalebone ship
sets her bones true.

Her heart speeds across
the figure in the mirror, returns
and admires the reflection
that has come far from its pallor.

She has given up her name for this.
It has taken much,

from brickyard and country songs and docks,
where she once held herself up
to be no more than a fish
swimming tight circles
in a pool beyond touch.

CINDERELLA

Laurel Johanson

The first time I saw Cinderella I was scraping crusted grease off the deep fryer at two minutes to midnight.

Fatty Patty was known for getting a few weirdos in the odd hours of the evening, but you're asking for it when you're a fast food joint open 24 hours a day. Every night I could add at least one person to the list of crazy characters I've encountered, and yeah, I actually do keep a list. I have a separate one for crazy um, "incidents," though. Like this one time an old man walked in and ordered two chocolate milkshakes but then as soon as he got them he just threw them on the floor and started writhing around in the mess, like some kid making snow angels at Christmas.

Sometimes regular customers ask how it is that our walls stay so white, almost *clinically* white, like a doctor's office or something, and I'd like to tell them it's because I personally scrub them down every night under my manager Eleanor's orders. It's really no wonder at all. But, of course, I don't say anything. I mostly just smile. "Let the guests think the elves did the cleaning while they were asleep," Eleanor would say. "And don't let them see *you* doing it." She says you should never shatter their illusions if you can help it. I try to laugh when she makes that same joke about the elves every night, but I smile at Eleanor the same way I do at the customers.

Cinderella came in on Halloween night wearing a full blue ball gown and tiara like she'd walked straight out of a fairy-tale. Sometimes when it gets really late, the bright fluorescence pulsating from those ugly tubes in the ceiling messes with my eyes, so when she walked in that night I had to quickly look behind me into our scratched stainless-steel kitchen to remind myself that yes, I was still in the depths of teenage hell and I hadn't been magically transported into a kids' movie.

I hadn't worn a costume to work that night but I figured wearing my uniform every day was dressing up enough, pretending my name was something like Little Miss Peppy Personable happily working the cash register for minimum wage until the ass-crack of dawn. Behind Cinderella some guy dressed as a giant lizard slithered in and put his arm around her waist. As soon as I saw him I thought, well there's another one for the list.

"Happy Halloween, bitches!" He yelled as soon as he entered. I couldn't help but think what a poor substitute for Prince Charming this intoxicated reptile was.

"Who are they?" My co-worker Karlee asked after she saw me staring.

"I don't know."

"She makes a gorgeous Cinderella. Not sure about that lizard-douche she's making out with though."

I tried my best not to pay attention to that lizard's tongue snaking in and out of Cinderella's mouth as I walked up to the counter to greet them.

"Hi there! What can I get for you?"

I counted five Mississippis before their mouths finally detached and she turned to look at me.

"Sorry, we just need a few," Cinderella answered, shooting a glance toward the lizard-man. He had made his way over to the drink machine behind her, looking like he was dangerously close to sticking his whole head underneath and trying to have a sip.

"You going to a party?" Karlee asked Cinderella from over my shoulder.

"Yeah," Cinderella smiled. "Off to the ball I guess you could say."

"It's already midnight though," I piped up. "Cinderella would be heading home by now."

"Oh," she gave me an odd look, like a kind of half-smile, half-frown. "Are you telling me to go home?"

"No," I replied hastily, and promptly scurried off to refill the ketchup stands after one of the most awkward silences of my life. I could see Karlee laughing at me from the corner of my eye. Traitor.

Lizard-man was still by the drink machine when I heaved my big bag of ketchup over to the condiment counter. He watched me work with a weird glint in his eyes, and I instinctively knew that lizard-man wouldn't *just* be going on my list tonight. I was probably going to have to write a whole diary entry dedicated to his shenanigans. At the time though, I tried to just keep my head down and work.

That didn't turn out so good for me.

"I've never seen so much ketchup in my life," he said quietly, his eyes widening. As for me, I'd never seen anyone's pupils so large in *my* life.

"It's just ketchup," I replied.

"It's like for when you're hungry *and* thirsty. It's like… so perfect."

I tried to ignore him, hoping that Cinderella would order a burger or something else to satisfy his munchies. Gorging on ketchup never did anyone any good. Unfortunately, I've seen plenty of evidence of that.

"Give it to me," he said suddenly.

"Huh?"

Before I knew what was happening, lizard-man lunged toward me and grabbed for my bag of ketchup. My grip on the bag automatically tightened out of reflex and so naturally the bag ripped wipe open as he pulled it from me, splattering ketchup on the floor and all over my uniform too. The lizard-man barely seemed to notice as he ran toward the bathroom with the bag of ketchup clutched to his chest like a newborn.

"What the FUCK?!" Karlee yelled from behind the front counter. Cinderella turned around and stared in horror at the sight of the ketchup-stained floor. Her eyes followed the red trail her lizard companion had left behind on his way to the bathroom.

"What the fuck," Cinderella echoed Karlee's words. She started toward the bathroom, but stopped and turned to me first. Her mouth opened as her eyes scanned my mess of a uniform, but it looked like she couldn't put any words to what she'd just witnessed.

"It's okay," I said, even though she hadn't actually apologized to me, and even though I liked ketchup a whole lot less than the lizard-man apparently did and the smell of it all over my body was already starting to make me sick.

Cinderella marched toward the men's room, and Karlee and I followed suit, Karlee with a mop and bucket in tow. We opened the bathroom door to find the lizard-man weeping on the floor, the bag in his lap and ketchup smeared all over the bathroom sink.

"Brett! What the hell?" Cinderella yelled. *Brett*. He'd always be lizard-douche to me and Karlee.

"I can't do this with you anymore," he said. "I looked in the mirror and I didn't like who I saw!"

"No shit," Cinderella said. "You're high as fuck, drenched in ketchup and wearing a *costume*."

"Well then what's *her* costume?" He pointed an accusatory finger at me.

"Is that why you covered her in ketchup, asshole?" Karlee yelled.

"I'm so sorry," Cinderella finally apologized to me. She pulled out her phone and started furiously texting. "Brett, your brother is coming to get you. You have to go wait outside for him."

"I'm not moving," he told her. "Tell him he'll have to drag me out if he wants!"

Karlee, still brandishing the mop, suddenly dunked the mop head into the bucket of soapy water and slapped Brett across the face with it.

"Ow!" He lifted his arms to shield his face, but Karlee was having none of it.

"Get out!" She yelled, as she prepared to dunk the mop into the water again.

He finally rose from the floor and fled the bathroom, but not before Karlee got a few more good hits in. She was so relentless I had to duck so as not to get sprayed with soapy water myself.

"I'd better go tell Eleanor about this." Karlee set the mop down, out of breath, and headed toward the manager's office.

"Wow," said Cinderella, wiping a drop of dirty water from her cheek. She turned to me, almost bashful. "Uh, I'm really sorry about all this. Is there anything I can do? Can I help you clean up, or—"

"No," I said maybe a little too quickly. I couldn't bring myself to meet her gaze after everything. "No, thanks."

Cinderella looked down at her shoes. I was glad to see they were ketchup-free, unlike mine, but they certainly weren't made of glass either. White sneakers. It was kind of cute.

"Anyway," I continued, "Cinderella's already late for the ball."

She looked up. "Well, Cinderella doesn't have a date anymore."

"Taking a lizard as a date was always a gamble."

I thought maybe I'd gone too far. I didn't know anything about their relationship after all. But Cinderella laughed, and the sound was so wonderful I couldn't help but laugh along with her. It wasn't anything like the way I usually laughed in front of customers.

"You've got me there," she said. "But you know how it is. Boys, am I right?"

I managed to smile a little even though I'd never had a boy in my life and never wanted to.

"Six months in and they can still just check out on you," she continued.

I thought about my parents, and how I'd grown up knowing that even sixteen *years* didn't mean someone would be yours forever.

"I think he was cheating on me," she said with a smile. I stopped smiling. "He was my ride to the party though. I mean, before he got wasted."

"Don't you have someone else that can take you?"

"Oh sure," she said. "No date though, like I said."

I shuffled in my shoes, uncomfortably aware in that moment of how completely covered in ketchup I truly was.

"Hey," Cinderella said suddenly. "Do you wanna come?"

"What?"

"To the party."

I stared at her for a few moments. "I'm not off until four."

She grinned. "What, being covered in ketchup isn't a good enough excuse to get off early?"

My stomach sank at the thought of approaching Eleanor with the subject. There wasn't anyone to cover my shift, we were understaffed enough as it was, plus I really needed the money and I wasn't going to know anyone at this party besides Cinderella. "I'll try," I found myself telling her, despite all the excuses I'd just made for myself.

"Cool," Cinderella said. "Well you should stop by and have a drink with me. Hopefully that'll make up for some of this mess. How long is this gonna take to clean anyway?"

I took a good long look at the bathroom. "Twenty minutes."

"Wow, that's it?"

"That's it."

Cinderella laughed. "Well I still feel bad. I feel like I owe you."

So pay me back, I almost found myself saying.

"Oh," she said after a few seconds. "Here's the address."

I watched as she went into one of the bathroom stalls and returned with two squares of toilet paper. She reached into her purse and searched unsuccessfully for a pen before pulling out a thin black eyeliner pencil.

"This'll have to do," Cinderella said as she scribbled an address onto the flimsy toilet paper squares. She handed them to me. "Careful, that's probably gonna smudge."

"Thanks," was all I could say.

"I'll see you later," she said as she walked out the men's room door. I thought I saw her wink at me as she left, but I knew that might've just been wishful thinking. Or those damn, ugly fluorescent lights.

* * *

True to my word, exactly twenty minutes later I abandoned the mop in the bathroom and made my way to Eleanor's office. When I opened the door, I saw her sitting in her chair filling out paperwork and eating multigrain crackers out of a plastic bag, one by one. Judging by the presence of the crackers, it was a bad time to come knocking.

"Hi Eleanor," I started lamely, "Some guy spilled ketchup all over me tonight. I thought maybe I could go home early?"

Eleanor didn't even look up from her papers. "Karlee told me. But I can't let you go home just for that." *Crunch*. "You understand." *Crunch*. "Wash up and get back to work."

"But I'm completely drenched— "

"Isabella," Eleanor cut me off. "You haven't even finished your tasks for this evening, have you?" *Crunch*. "Did you mop?"

"Yes, so did Karlee." In a sense, Karlee *did* mop.

"And did you—" *Crunch*. "—restock the cups and the cutlery and the ketchup like I asked?"

"Well I *tried* to."

Eleanor zipped up her bag of crackers with her thumb and index finger and turned to look at me. "And what about the fryer, did you degrease it?"

"I—I just finished it," I stuttered.

"Well do it again. And then you can start cleaning the gum out from under the patio tables."

"But it's freezing outside— "

"Isabella, just do your job. And I'd better not see you clock out of here even one minute before four."

I left the office in a daze and headed for the walk-in refrigerator at the back of the kitchen. There were no cameras in there, so it was common for Fatty Patty employees to take our frustrations to the fridge, out of Eleanor's sight. Two years working under Eleanor meant that the fridge and I had become very close companions.

Tears that I didn't even know had started forming were already running down my cheeks, so I reached into my pocket and wiped them away with Cinderella's crumpled toilet paper note. *50 Nightingale Lane.* The wetness caused the words to bleed together. Now it was just another dirty tissue. I sighed and started to cry freely, collapsing onto a food crate on the floor.

Eventually Karlee found me as she often did. She pulled up a crate beside me and put her head on my shoulder. She found the tissue clenched tightly in my first and gently dabbed my cheeks.

"I'm sorry that douche spilled ketchup all over you."

"I don't care about him," I said quietly.

Karlee frowned. "Izzy, what is it?"

I explained to her about Cinderella's invitation and Eleanor's refusal to let me leave, or even change clothes. Karlee listened and I could tell she understood that it wasn't just about missing the party, or the ketchup, or even our shitty boss.

"Well," Karlee said, "That settles it. Now you *have* to go."

"I can't. Eleanor said… and I don't even have anything to wear—"

"No no no." Karlee held up her hand. "Leave everything to me."

She exited the fridge, but materialized a few minutes later with a shimmery purple dress and black heels in her hands.

"I wore this as a bridesmaid a few days ago. You're lucky I'm lazy and still had these stuffed in my trunk. Here, try them on."

"I'll just get them dirty," I said.

"Well then take off your gross ketchup uniform and we'll work from there."

So I started to strip in the middle of the refrigerator, grateful to shed my uniform and the awful memories of the lizard-man along with it. Karlee carefully slipped the dress over my head, and I forced my feet into the little black heels.

"Well, the dress is a little loose," Karlee said. "But I can fix that."

"Can you make the shoes two sizes bigger?"

"That I can't do," she replied. "But if you wear the shoes to the party you can just ditch them when you get there right? Here, hold still while I pin this."

I had no idea where Karlee had been hiding those safety pins or how she was managing to make all of this possible. But she was, and I had no words for how grateful I felt. Still one thing was casting a shadow over Karlee's efforts, though.

"How am I gonna explain this to Eleanor?" I asked.

"Oh, don't worry," Karlee said, while cleaning ketchup out of my hair with brown paper towel. "Eleanor's not nearly as squeaky clean as she makes out. I have... proof."

I shuddered. "Please don't say any more."

Karlee gave me a devilish smirk. "Well then, off you go! It's already quarter to one." She ushered me out of the fridge, but stopped us for a moment in the doorway. "Izzy, try and have fun tonight okay? I'm *rooting* for you."

I smiled at my friend and hugged her goodbye. "Thank you."

"You smell like ketchup still," she whispered in my ear. "Bye!"

* * *

I cabbed for 25 minutes to get to Nightingale Lane but spent another fifteen minutes with my cab driver out front debating whether or not to actually go inside.

"You getting out?" He asked me.

I didn't respond at first. I was fidgeting in my heels that were already blistering my feet even though I'd barely even walked in them.

"Maybe I'll just go back," I told him, though I was still staring at the house out the cab window.

"You came all this way," he said. "Why would you want to go back?"

In the end, I pictured Karlee beating that lizard guy's ass with a wet mop and decided that if she could do that for me, I could at least walk up the steps and through the front door past a few drunk strangers for her sake. My cab fare ended up being more than my entire night's wages because of my stalling, but I decided it was worth it when I saw her running up to me in the warm, golden glow of the fairy lights draped across the archway to the living room.

"It's you!" Cinderella said. "I barely recognized you!"

"Is that good or bad?" I asked her.

"You cleaned up good," she said, smiling. "I like your dress. What are you supposed to be?"

"Huh?"

"Your costume," she said. "Did you forget it's Halloween?"

"Oh." I honestly had. "I guess I'm a bridesmaid."

"I wonder if Cinderella had bridesmaids at her wedding," she said seriously.

She took my arm and we ventured deeper into the 70's-style home to its turquoise linoleum kitchen. Cinderella bypassed the glass punch bowl and went straight for an amber-coloured bottle, pouring a shot each into two little red cups.

"Bottoms up," she said as she handed one to me. I did mine over the sink because I'd only started drinking last year when I turned 17 and hard liquor didn't agree with me yet.

"Dance with me?" Cinderella asked, while I was still grimacing from my whiskey-burned throat.

"Yeah," my voice cracked like a little boy's. She laughed and lead me to a crowded wood-panelled living room with orange shag carpet and an old record player with a glass case in the corner. Music was coming from somewhere else, a phone probably, but the record player put a goofy smile on my face for some reason. It made me feel almost nostalgic, but that made no sense because I wasn't even alive in the 70s. Maybe it was just the liquor and Cinderella's hands on my shoulders giving me that warm longing for a place I'd never been before.

"You took way longer than 20 minutes," she yelled over the music.

"I got a little lost," I tried to tell her.

She didn't hear me. "What?"

I smiled and shook my head, and we danced until I realized I was still wearing those ridiculous heels. Cinderella knelt down in front of me in her dress and helped me slip them off, laughing and throwing them over her shoulder when she did.

Two hours and three more shots later, I became even more convinced that hard liquor didn't agree with me.

"What's wrong?" Cinderella yelled, her hands secure on my shoulders while we swayed.

"I'm gonna lie down," I responded, reluctantly waving her hands away.

I stumbled down the long hallway, dizzied by the green floral wallpaper, and managed to find the nearest bed. I didn't realize at first was that it was already occupied by dozens of coats, but I found them oddly comforting and decided to nestle right into the pile. I thought of that weird old man that had writhed around in the milkshakes back at Fatty Patty. Maybe I'd make it onto someone else's crazy list one of these days. Maybe I already had. I burrowed deeper and deeper until all I saw was black. It reminded me a little of when I used to hide in my closet when I was younger while my parents fought. The darkness had always helped clear my head for some reason. Maybe because it's easier to think when your problems aren't right there staring you in the face. Maybe that was cowardly of me to think that way.

I felt someone lie down on the bed beside me, so I poked my head out. Cinderella was lying on her back staring at something on the ceiling. She turned her head toward me, and screamed as soon as she saw my face among the coats. Her screams quickly turned to laughter, though. She perched herself on her elbows and looked down at me.

"Are you hiding?" She asked, poking my face with warm fingers.

"Stop that," I said, swatting her hand away. "I'm not hiding." *Not anymore. Not from you.*

"Were you passed out? Well pardon me then, Sleeping Beauty." She snuggled up beside me on the pile of coats. "Wow, this is... actually pretty cozy."

We lie there for a few minutes like that until I convinced myself she'd finally had enough of me, had probably fallen asleep beside me, wouldn't remember anything about me in the morning.

"What's your name?" She finally asked in barely a whisper. I felt her warm whiskey breath on my neck, so I turned my head.

"Isabella," I said, as her fingers grazed my chin. I took her hand in mine and laced those fingers with my own.

She turned to look at the clock beside us on the bed, then looked back at me. "It's 3:33, Isabella. Make a wish."

"I wish I'd kissed Cinderella at midnight."

"There's still time," she said. "I haven't turned into a pumpkin yet."

"That's actually not what happens in the story," I tried to explain, but she kissed me, so I took that to mean she didn't really care for fairy-tales anyway.

SHEATH!

Mary Panke

The dress drops over her head like she is diving into a pool,
first recognition in the mirror a long loud O, like oxygen.

I square her shoulders and zip, up, the back, run my hands down
her waist, hips, thighs, so pleasing I do it again, like I'm swiping

away water, clearing away years of ill-fitting clothes in dingy
dressing rooms as her body morphed from muscular limbs to
tender pillows, rounded

and queer. Sheathing unsheathes, brings out the babe in black boots
rising up on the balls of her feet, eyes wide, mouth wide,

she is a warrior queen, she is Captain Janeway in a dress
and today I am whooping, today I am wet like water.

SHERLOCK HOLMES AND THE CIRCUS

Adjie Henderson

May 25, 1903

"Dear Mycroft,

It seems only yesterday that I took pen to paper to write about the death of your brother and my dear friend, Sherlock Holmes. My previous accounts involving his death were woefully inadequate due to the sorrow I felt.

As you are aware, Holmes and I were estranged for a time since I succumbed to my parents' dictates to enter a proper marriage and encourage my medical practice. Obviously, the intimate relations existing between dear Holmes and myself became strained. We met from time to time, mostly because he wished companionship as he worked on his various investigations.

After my wife died, Holmes and I made a trip to the continent. We spent some time in France and Germany, hiking and enjoying the lovely food and wine in the hostels of the area. It was on this trip that I became convinced Professor Moriarty murdered Holmes. Holmes and Moriarty, locked in mortal combat, fell over a cliff and into the rushing water of a waterfall. Nothing remained of Holmes except his hiking stick and a letter addressed to me. I gather the letter was written days before and dropped at the scene. I confess I revised the letter in my public accounts. The letter was of a privileged nature and the real contents will remain confidential.

I feel compelled to clarify some of my earlier versions without disturbing the general perception of excellence associated with dear old Holmes. The enclosed manuscript is a beginning and should provide you with an account of events that occurred most recently. None of these will add to his acclaim as a brilliant mind. Rather, they will serve as milestones as our lives forever change.

Yours sincerely,

John H. Watson, Doctor of Medicine"

* * *

A Return to the Continent

I remained in my office late on one of those dreadfully cold nights in London when it is difficult to muster the courage to go home. My medical notes were seriously interrupted by a loud scratch from the window. I looked up and saw nothing and attributed the scratching to a cat. I was, after all, tired from a long day in my clinic and wished to write a few words before going to our old apartment, having dinner and falling asleep in my chair by the fire. The scratching continued and I opened the window, opaque from the dingy London air, to encourage the cat to leave me be. But as the window opened, a human figure appeared, presenting itself in increasing horizontal fragments as I raised the filthy glass. Holmes stood proudly in the alleyway, a scarf covering most of his face in a makeshift disguise. He climbed through the window and stood watching my disbelieving face.

"I assure you I am not a ghost, Watson," he announced. "Indeed, I am very alive. It is time we took a short trip to appease an old friend."

"Of course," I said. "I have been such a bore lately. But are you well, other than you are supposed to be dead? "

"Obviously, I am not dead," Holmes said, "although I had thoughts about my demise on my way down the cliff. Indeed, I was somewhat bruised, but I fell onto a ledge with the brunt of the fall taken by my backpack which we filled with all sorts of soft stuff including the pillows and cloths for our picnic."

"But where is Moriarty?" I asked.

"I have no idea, but we should leave England. We will go to Paris since my friend there is in need. Perhaps we will go to a circus. It will do you good to get away."

"Yes, indeed. I was beginning to suspect my sanity. Your syringe and other apparatuses were missing from the mantle and I am sure Mrs. Hudson would never touch them. At least I have some explanation for this phenomenon. I assume you came into the apartment while we were occupied elsewhere?"

"Indeed," said Holmes, "and I removed much more including a bottle of absinthe."

We disguised ourselves for the train trip. I wore workman's clothes and Holmes sported a keffiyeh. Holmes's friend, introduced only as Sebastian, greeted us warmly at Gare du Nord.

Sebastian, assuredly greater than six feet in height, walked rapidly towards us, his arms outstretched in greeting. He was a foppish guy, dressed in an extravagant manner. His gilded jacket would be described as in bad taste in London but he covered it with a magnificent cape of multiple colors. His blue silk pantaloons were tucked into high brown leather boots. He held a broad brim hat in his hand and looked as if he had arrived late for a tea party.

I realized soon enough this was his usual attire. Indeed, he was rather effeminate for such a big fellow, but his humor led me to forget his excesses. We retreated to his hotel for warmth and decided to continue our stay in the hotel's lovely rooms. The fireplace in the parlor was a welcome sight and they drank absinthe. I nursed an excellent Calvados which only the French seemed to have.

"Now, we should discuss the circus," said Holmes, "and you can explain, dear Sebastian."

"Not much of course, but my friend works there. He will show us around tomorrow. It will be a fun trip."

A speeding carriage almost struck Holmes as we left our hotel. I became immediately alarmed and pulled him out of harm's way, but he appeared not to notice. Sebastian chased the driver, still traveling at an amazing speed, throwing his fist up with some less than savory words.

"You drivers are idiots and should not be allowed on the streets of Paris."

It was surely the work of Moriarty.

We arrived to the excitement and planned mayhem of a circus returning to its home base. The tent wagons formed a circle around a large circus building, making a boundary between the brilliant colors of the circus and the outside world. The clowns came outside, all made up for their makeshift show and encouraged us to come back for the big evening event.

We did not find Sebastian's friend Franco. Rather, we found Franco's wife Bianca in their wagon. She looked up from her stool as we entered the tiny space.

She was crying,

"Franco is dead. He fell, but his fall was no accident."

* * *

A Statement of the Case

"It wasn't an accident," Bianca repeated over and over. "Something is wrong here. He has been up and down the rope ladder for years. The police were convinced he became dizzy from taking morphine in his tea, a common circus remedy. He doesn't take drugs, medical or otherwise and he doesn't drink tea.

"My friend is dead?" questioned an unbelieving Sebastian. "My tower of strength in this world of evil is gone. He also knew excellent sources of various opiates at reasonable prices."

"Are you sure it was foul play?" Holmes asked. "There may be danger for you. We should call the local Gendarme."

"The police were here," she said. "There was nothing to tell them."

"Who would want to kill him?" I asked.

Holmes glanced at me with his eyebrows raised, "That is for us to determine. We cannot simply speculate."

He seemed to be studying the walkway as we strolled to the circus building. He was obviously upset, surprisingly so since I assumed he had never met Franco. Inside what I perceived as a round building was really a polygon with seats for spectators placed in the open spaces between columns. The accident could have been observed from any vantage point in the building, but apparently no one had done so, or come forth.

Holmes walked through the building and rather foolishly, I thought for his age, climbed the rope ladder. His skills and facilities have remained of course, excellent, but he had agreed to curtail his activities in light of his physical condition. He appeared to be driven to frenzy in his effort to determine what happened and spent some time measuring and calculating angles of descent.

A small wide-eyed group from the freak show watched him. I ventured to speak to a few of them, but they were quite shy. I asked a tiny woman about their work schedule.

Holmes interrupted with the obvious question, "Did any of you see the accident?"

The tiny woman held the hand of a woman with an enormous amount of facial hair. Then the group walked away as silently as when they entered.

"It is difficult for them in public," explained Bianca. "They stay mostly among themselves."

Later, I returned from my afternoon walk through Paris to our rooms where Holmes and Sebastian sat quietly smoking opium-tainted Egyptian cigarettes. We chatted amicably and commiserated with Sebastian on the loss of his friend.

"The venders in the circus area are the best source of cocaine, morphine or hashish," he recalled. "There is a problem with finding such drugs these days unless you find cough syrup palatable. We will have to resort to cognac or absinthe or have the good doctor here write us medical permission."

"No, indeed not," I said in my professional voice. "These chemicals are bad for the brain processes. I have told Holmes stories of the horrible effects of cocaine or hashish on the body. It did not deter his activities, however."

"The local officials don't seem to be worried about our health," said Sebastian. "I suspect the they are more worried about the demise of the proud French language and customs than the general health of the populace, particularly among the lower classes."

In this peaceful setting, a shot rang out and entered the open window of the parlor in our suite, striking the very chair where Holmes had just leaned forward to fetch a glass of cognac teasingly presented by Sebastian. I ran to the window, but there was no one there— only a carriage racing away.

"Yes," Holmes said, calmly considering his cognac, "We were recognized. Earlier I noted footsteps behind us mimicking our pace by slowing down and speeding up when we did. I did not dare look around, but I suspect we would all have recognized our follower as Professor Moriarty."

As he spoke we heard a knock at the door and the landlord presented Holmes with a rather formal-looking letter. He took the envelope, held it up to the light, and carefully studied all the sides and the flap.

"It's Moriarty's distinct writing style. There is a flourish on the S of Sherlock."

He read the letter quietly and then turned to us reading aloud,

"My dear Sherlock,

You cannot get rid of me so simply. As you will recall, I spent vacations in those mountains as a youth and no one knows the area as I do. There is a deep pool under the falls. If one lands correctly from the rock above there is no harm done other than a thorough soaking in extremely cold water. Unfortunately, your fall was broken by the ledge. You seem none the worse for wear, however.

I have business here and a lovely apartment. I assumed you would be with Sebastian as he insists on calling himself. I see you have brought the ratty little doctor along as a cover for your activities most of which I find distasteful, but your addictions help keep me quite well funded for other enterprises.

Stay away from Sebastian.

Prof. Moriarty."

"What is he talking about?" I asked, looking at all in amazement.

No answer came from either of the men. Holmes retired to an easy chair and quietly smoked a pipe containing hashish.

We attended the circus in the evening. We kept in the shadows. Our disguises were useless, and besides, Sebastian's casual wear for the circus was definitely colorful.

A full house of cheering people enjoyed the show. I caught myself uncharacteristically clapping with my fellow viewers at the sight of insane people standing on the back of galloping horses and wild animals jumping through hoops. The acrobats flew through the air with only a rough net and some mattresses below them.

"A most spectacular display," I mentioned to Sebastian and Holmes. "I have never seen such an exciting show."

Holmes did not hear me. He appeared to be disinterested, but he looked into space, and talked to no one in particular.

"Indeed, there should have been a net in the area where Franco fell. He would probably still be alive if the net and mattresses had been there."

"Perhaps Franco slipped outside the net," a slight possibility I admitted to myself, "or perhaps someone moved the netting either inadvertently or on purpose."

"Maybe," said Holmes. "The rope ladder is always in place. Perhaps someone weakened the rungs near the top or oiled them. The next person up would simply wipe away the grease as well as possible. Climbing these ladders is not a job for an amateur. I found it to be a bit unnerving, but any of the acrobats could be enticed to climb with no anxiety."

* * *

The Tragedy of the Dark House

After our trip to the circus Holmes disappeared for several days. I was happy to roam the city at will and visit some hospitals. In my travels, I met the attending doctor at the hospital where they took Franco and questioned him concerning the medical facts.

"It is strange," he ventured, "since you are the second person to ask me about this. I don't remember the man's name-a strange fellow wearing a keffiyeh. As I mentioned to him, Franco flew straight down in a dive and landed on his head. By landing on his head he broke his neck immediately."

"A most unpleasant death, but I can determine the facts soon, along with my friend Sherlock Holmes who I believe you met yesterday," I announced to an impressed physician who was aware of Sherlock Holmes, even here in France!

I returned to our quiet rooms. Sebastian left earlier to attend to business. Apparently he is a writer of some variety and has a play in progress. A note waited for me.

"Mr. Holmes mentioned I should give you this if he wasn't back by the third day of his absence," said the proprietor. "I assume he is well. I observed he was not eating well."

Fearful of ill-play, I rushed to the address on the note, a house called La Petite Maison des Garçons. Our carriage flew by the people of the evening drinking wine and dancing to cabaret music. The scene became shabbier as reached our journey to the edge of Paris. Curly haired young men dressed in clothes even more effeminate than those Sebastian wore were prowling the streets. The gas lights had not yet been replaced in this desolate spot and they flickered in the wind causing the shadows to come alive.

The house I sought was located in an underpass, in a place even darker than the streets above. I asked the driver to wait and made my way down the well- worn steps toward the lights of a decrepit rooming house. A yellowish haze of opium smoke filled the house and there were bodies, like large dolls, lying across each piece of aged furniture. The shadows of men and young boys holding each other in the dark smoke-filled bedrooms were everywhere. After a failure to find Holmes, I rushed outside with every intention of ridding myself of this house forever. A woman in ragged clothes stopped me, holding her hand out for coins left in the men's pockets.

She followed me out screaming, "A well-dressed person such as yerself should cough up a few coins for a poor widow."

I guessed at once the voice belonged to Holmes. Once we were away from the building, he removed his disguise.

"I see you have been in the clinics again today, Watson."

"How can you tell? I venture to guess you have spent your days in this horrid place."

"You have a spot of colored antiseptic on your finger and a pair of rubber surgical gloves in your pocket. Also you smell like carbolic acid. Indeed it is a simple deduction."

"You were here?" I asked.

"I came here tonight to bring Sebastian back to his room," answered Holmes. "The place is filled with peedy types and young boys who perform sex for money and drugs. This is one of the places owned by Moriarty, but more on this later. I found Sebastian, but he would not leave. He kept saying, 'the only way to cure my soul is to give in to the senses. The best way I can do that is to buy forgetfulness with opium.'"

"I will return for him," I said. "You should not be seen."

As I made my way through the narrow hallway, a tall figure bent its way out of a bed and I saw Sebastian, unshaven, dirty and quite pale,

"Good day, my good Watson. I assume you have come to fetch me? Is it late?"

"Almost six."

"Good, then we will be on time for Wednesday wine at the cabaret."

"It's Friday."

"That's lovely. Then we are on time for Friday wine."

I put us in the cab with instructions to the driver to rush us back to the hotel. In the interim, Holmes disappeared again somewhere into the dark streets. I returned to the circus area in an attempt to find him. The employees were off for the evening and the grounds were almost deserted.

I made my way to Bianca's wagon where the open tent door revealed a shadow of her sitting on her stool reflected by the candle light. She was quite a beautiful woman as if recorded in a painting by Renoir. My feelings at the moment were not something I would ever discuss with Mrs. Watson, a typical English wife. The Spanish and French women have a quiet romance about them, an aura of something possible but might never happen.

"Good evening," I said trying to be professional, "are you quite alright?"

We spoke for a while on innocuous subjects and I stayed for the night. We awoke early to a bright sun shining through the tent door. We were both better, not because of some illicit romance, but rather because it was a peaceful time.

* * *

The Case Darkens

"Franco knew more than I told you," she blurted out as we ate our bread and coffee, "and so did I. I should have spoken up earlier. A serious problem exists with the Spanish lads working with the circus. They are being prostituted."

"There are many reasons to have young men around a circus," I sympathized.

"They are children from some little village in rural Spain," she explained. "I cleaned them up and made sure they were properly dressed. I, too, assumed they would work as laborers on the circus grounds. Now they sell everything in their tent wagons from hashish to sex. Once they are addicted to drugs, they have to sell their bodies to buy more drugs, as well as send monies back to their village."

"How on earth did they get here?"

"They came with the Spanish acrobats. They got to Paris by crossing the border hidden somewhere in the circus junk."

"I visited the house of the rent boys to recover Sebastian," I confided. "It is a filthy place filled with opium smoke. I assume many of the boys there are from the Spanish group."

"Yes, many are from the circus," said Bianca. "The acrobats convinced everyone they were bringing help to their family's village. Initially they brought five of the local lads to the circus. They lived so far back in the Spanish countryside that they came part of the way by donkey. Then they were given train tickets to Madrid where they met the circus. They had nothing but the clothes on their backs."

"Do they have papers?" I asked. "There must be 20 or so boys here now."

Bianca hesitated as if she heard something and then continued, "The boys are dressed in clown outfits. When they cross the border, the number of papers, legal or not, matches the number of clowns."

"I gather someone is making a lot of money?"

"Oh yes, including the boys' families. On the last trip to Spain, we were suddenly awash in young boys ready and willing to come to the circus."

"And Franco knew this?"

"Yes, but he had no idea of the extent of the problem. None of us questioned anything initially. It is the way of life in the circus. It came together when one of the boys, Emanuel, from the original group recognized his brother Rico in the new group of arrivals. He would do anything to be able to send money to his impoverished family, but did not want his brother involved. He came to Franco."

"So Franco became a confidante for the boys?"

"Yes, but he was already suspicious. Franco became depressed when he realized the part he played in the drug and sex trade. Now he is gone and they will kill me next."

I heard a rustling and in a moment a familiar figure crawled through the rear of the tent. Holmes had arrived. I hoped he would be discreet.

"I am glad you have heard all," he said, "but you took a chance to come here. I am in grave danger and I do not wish the same for you. People who commit immoral acts would have no mercy for us."

Bianca continued her story,

"Everyone loved Franco. We met 5 years ago in Madrid where I sang in one of the cabaret shows. He stopped drugs when we married. He did not want to return as an acrobat so he became a manager for the

238

circus building. The person responsible for bringing the boys here is the head acrobat, Carlos Ramirez, but I have no legal proof."

"Surely there is someone who can confirm what you are saying," I said.

"The family would never speak against him. They have been a part of a circus for at least three generations. Families have to get along. You live together, work together and eat together and either sleep together or in proximity. You would not swing on a trapeze through the air into the arms of someone you did not like or someone who was angry with you."

I tried to comfort Bianca. Before we left, we promised to take care of Emanuel and his brother or any of the boys who we could entice to leave the circus.

* * *

In Pursuit of a Solution

"How can we prove Ramirez is the guilty person?" I asked as we walked through the city.

"I am not ready to say," explained Holmes. "We must tread carefully. Most of the circus performers were born into a special lifestyle, one on the far fringes of what we have defined of as a normal society. For a few magic moments, they astound us and then the spotlight is off, the makeup is removed and they retreat into their cramped tent trailers. Breaking into their world, even for a moment, seems impossible. They are used to dangerous tasks. As I told you, anyone who is capable of causing addiction in youths would not hesitate to slit your throat."

I admit I had not considered the full consequences of our little investigation. We walked slowly making a circuitous route along the Seine. He was uncharacteristically considerate. Perhaps he had softened a bit with age.

"I, too, am sickened by young boys becoming addicted to opiates, but it is not illegal for them to have sexual relations with older men at their age. The age of consent here is 13. These kinds of relationships are certainly not a new phenomenon. Historically, they have been considered quite normal."

"Medically, I am more worried about venereal diseases than morality," I countered.

We returned to spend some time over evening drinks discussing the rent boys. I rocked in my oversized chair by the fire while Sebastian stretched his long frame over a chaise lounge. Homes sat quietly in the Morris chair looking out the window to the street.

"Obviously we should spend some time observing the activities of the boys," I suggested. "It is possible we can get enough information on Carlos Ramirez or whoever to have them arrested."

"Consider first their conditions," advised Holmes. "Some of their money goes to their families but most goes to the Spanish acrobats. None of the boys has enough funds to escape the circus and certainly not enough to pay their way home. By the way, from observing their duties, they assuredly cannot plan on circus preforming as means of obtaining a living."

"They have learned nothing about the circus," said Sebastian. "When they are not working as rent boys, they are dressed in usher costumes and prance around carrying flags, hardly an invaluable talent."

"We have to concentrate on what can be defined as illegal," said Holmes. "The Code Napoleon has ensured that since 1805, acts of sex between men in private are not criminal offenses."

"Surely this would not be true in England," I announced with pride.

Holmes grimaced, "The French, as well as the English, don't like homosexual activity, although it is tolerated. The English, however, can be overbearing, and even vindictive since it disobeys their religious beliefs and long ingrained customs."

"The English are evil bigots," said Sebastian. "British prejudice has many strange manifestations. They are stuffed full of titles and royalty,"

"Sebastian was incarcerated in England for homosexual activities," said Holmes.

Holmes continued his lecture,

"It is not just the legal or illegal we are dealing with. Not surprisingly some of the boys are fine with the arrangement. It would be difficult to convince them to leave. Consider their options, one of which would be leaving Paris to return to a dirt poor little village in the mountains."

"Of course, but this is still bondage," I said. "What happens when they are older? Are they just let go to roam the streets?"

"You are unfortunately correct," said Sebastian. "I see men of all ages dressed ridiculously as youths. They have on makeup in a futile attempt to hide the ravages of time. The amount they charge goes down and down and then there is nothing left but syphilis."

"And so to the point of legality," Holmes began to read. "Article 334 of the French Penal Code says 'whoever offends against morals by habitually inciting, abetting or facilitating the profligacy or interaction of the youth of either sex under the age of 21 years shall be punished from 6 months to a year.' If they are making money off young men's backs, it is illegal."

"The funds the boys receive for sex are collected by the brother of Ramirez," said Sebastian. "He is a burly guy who no longer does trapeze acts, but supplies his large number of sons for the show."

"How on earth do you find that out?" I asked.

"One of the boys told me."

"Can't we ask the boys to testify?"

"Only in secret," said Holmes. "Otherwise they would probably be dead before they had a chance to speak."

* * *

Trapping Moriarty

"Dear Watson," Holmes said, "as you have guessed from our conversations, the owner of the circus is Moriarty. Influencing young boys is not his style. There is someone else who is using his operations for immoral purposes and I will find out who it is."

"Moriarty is a crook," I noted, having no idea he owned the circus.

"You slander him by referring to him as a crook," said Holmes. "This is libel in his eyes. You forget he is a celebrated author of a brilliant mathematical treatise."

"A brilliant crook is still a crook," I noted as Sebastian shook his head in agreement.

"We are setting a trap for Mr. Ramirez. We must have positive proof that he is pocketing funds from this operation. My first step in this plan was to pester the local Morals Brigade. They are a bit of a shady bunch, but there are few good men. There is a chap there who looks quite young for his age and he is willing to apply for a circus job. Of course they could just close the house down or at least threaten to do so. I am sure they are getting paid off. More money and the threat of disclosing their less savory activities worked miracles."

"He must dress for the part," said Sebastian. "I have the perfect outfit."

Sebastian took over. When they returned Luc had on makeup and his waist was cinched to mimic a young woman's body. He was gorgeous. He carried a perfumed handkerchief in his hand, the signal the street boys use. The young officer also had a gun in a hidden pocket.

Luc left for the circus area where he requested an interview with the head acrobat. The following is his account of the events when we met later,

"I was rather taken back to be seen so soon by Mr. Ramirez. Apparently they needed fresh boys for his activities at La Petit Maison and hired me to report for work this evening. He and his brother decide how the funds are divided, but there are higher-ups somewhere. He informed me that any monies are handed over to them at exactly 10 pm."

"Don't worry," said Sebastian. "You will be my partner. Others you trust in the Brigade des Moeurs should also come as customers."

"Yes," said Holmes, "this will address the first issue—proof Mr. Ramirez is breaking the French penal code. Hopefully we will also be able to determine who is supplying the drugs, although it may turn out to be legal for at least the present time."

We arrived in different carriages and were discharged some distance from the disreputable house. Sebastian and a member of the brigade followed close behind Luc. Both were dressed in clothes I had never seen in England. Sebastian outdid himself.

Luc entered the house and given a room number by a man in an oriental costume. Another man with drugs sold him his nightly supply. Sebastian came to Luc's room where they sat for some time.

Holmes again disguised himself as an old woman begging coins from the clientele. At exactly 10 pm, the rooms were vacated. Any monies were turned over at the door. I waited patiently and watched to see who entered or left the building. Carlos Ramirez entered the building, appeared to check everything and left in the carriage with his brother. They were followed by the police.

One more person left the building, a man with a tall and thin stature, sunken eyes and a domed forehead with a shock of grey hair. The old woman portrayed by Holmes was being observed. The thin man raised his cane and laughed.

"You are ridiculous," he teased. "I will destroy you soon."

He raised a knife hidden within the cane towards Holmes's throat. Then he disappeared completely into the night. Holmes also disappeared, but arrived the next morning with a summary of events.

"Why were no arrests made?" I asked.

"These are the little people," said Holmes pompously. "We will use them as bait to find others throughout Europe."

We repeated our performances the next night and again the last person to exit was the tall gaunt man. The Morals squad traced the main suspects to a building near the circus, a business advertising pharmaceuticals products. On the third day, the Morals Squad raided the offices. The rooms were empty. The Spanish troupe of acrobats left the circus in the dark of night presumably to return to Spain. The Police dispatched a telegram to the border patrol and the Ramirez brothers were stopped at the border, brought back to Paris and are in jail awaiting the decision of the judge. It is probable they will just be exported to Spain, but they will no longer be able to practice their illicit activities in France. The Petit Maison was also raided and the boys were sent to a hospital for medical testing and withdrawal from drugs. Their bills were paid by an unknown benefactor.

Someone tipped off the Ramirez brothers. We later found out a member of the Brigade was paid liberally for his advice to the pharmaceutical owners. No one knows who else was involved.

* * *

Leaving the Continent

"Well Holmes, it's time for us to leave for London."

"It is time for you," he said. "Please arrange for Emanuel and Rico's trip to Sussex. They are refusing to return to Spain since their family doesn't want them. They are expected on the farm and will be assets since I need help with the bees."

"But surely you need rest."

"Of course, but for now I have to remain in Paris. Sebastian is ill. I am sure you as a physician have noticed his physical constitution."

"I assumed his habits were driving his poor physical condition," I said. "Can I be of use medically?"

"I fear it is too late," said Holmes. "Of course, I will find Moriarty. I am sure he is still in Paris."

"Moriarty and I were school chums," he ventured carefully. "As long as I am being straightforward with you, we were quite taken with each other in a boyish sort of way and were intimate for some years. He matched my intellect and I looked forward to each day after classes when we spent time together.

At some point as we grew older, I left him. I could not defend his churlish ways and at times he frightened me. He never forgave me. He threatened me and anyone I was close to. That includes you dear Watson, but he soon realized our relationship was in fact rather provincial. My relationship with Sebastian, however, totally brought him over the edge.

Sebastian had such a promising future as a classicist. He learned at least four foreign languages as a child. We were all educated at Trinity College, Dublin and later at Oxford. After the university, Sebastian moved to London and associated himself with fashionable cultural circles. He gave lecture tours dressed as 'Little Lord Fauntleroy'"

"His dress has changed little," I noted.

"He was a lover of a titled brat named Bosie. Bosie's father had him put in jail. When he got out, his reputation was destroyed and he changed his name and left for France."

I returned to our rooms feeling dejected that I was not their intellectual equal.

When Holmes returned, I asked to be updated on all fronts.

"Who killed Franco?"

"Suicide."

"But how did you determine that?"

"It had to be intentional," explained Holmes. "Only an acrobat with deliberate maneuvers would fall the way he did. He simply could not live with the thought of young boys becoming sex slaves and drug addicts."

"You have no proof."

"He was observed."

"Good heavens, you have witnesses!"

"The group from the freak show tent watched."

"What a horrible way to die," I said. "Why not take an overdose of something?"

"Perhaps it was his way of saying goodbye to the circus."

"And where is Moriarty?" I asked.

"He is on the way back to England. We will meet again soon."

I returned by train to London with the boys. I purchased some proper English clothes for them and placed them on the train to Sussex Downs where they would be met by a tutor and Mrs. Hudson for all to start their new lives. I buried myself in my medical practice for some days and then Bianca came to London.

Sebastian died a few weeks after I returned to London. Holmes later told me his last words, "This wallpaper and I are fighting a duel to the death. Either it goes or I do."

Holmes came back to London a changed man. He finally began to speak of retiring to his country home in Sussex Downs.

"Dear Holmes, it seems so unfair," I said. "You did the work, but I get a wife, the boys get a home and Moriarty is probably well somewhere in London. What is there for you?"

He reached his hand towards the mantel and picked up his syringe.

* * *

November 14, 1903

"Dear Mycroft.

I find myself in the rather strange position of having to revise my previous accounts of Holmes. Both he and Moriarty have convinced me that events I described did not occur as I wrote them.

My conundrum is that I suspect my stories had much more complicated plots than I recorded and now I am not sure my previous accounts were real. I hope you will help me make a decision as to revising previous journals and stories.

Thank you for your editorial help.

Yours truly,

John H. Watson"

* * *

Sherlock Holmes Retires

I received an invitation from Holmes to visit him at his farm in Sussex Downs. It is not a grandiose farm. There is a large cottage, a guest house and room enough for a small vegetable garden and his bee-keeping, a practice for which he is known worldwide. I arrived on an evening late in August. Below the lights of the ships reflected in the bay and I looked down to a broad sweep of beach at the foot of a chalk cliff. I was at peace.

The lamps of the cab faded in the distance as I stood transfixed before the great sea. Then rattling sounds and the blinding motor lamps of an oncoming car brought me back. A mechanized beast, part of the herds populating our roads, destroyed my peace.

The lights of the car came to a halt at the gate. A passenger hurried towards me swinging his briefcase. The chauffeur turned the car around and headed for a small garage in the distance.

"I so hoped I would make it back in time to pick you up at the station," the unknown gentleman said. "It's a beautiful night for a drive."

A tall thin man with sunken eyes observed me. In spite of his motoring outfit and goggles, I knew I had seen him before. Then it came to me. He was the last to leave each night from the house of the boys. As we both looked up at the strange multi-gabled house, Sherlock sprung down the pathway, pointed to the moonlit sea and motioned for us to enter.

"Turn around and meet my nemesis," said Holmes, "and life partner, James Moriarty."

The tall figure with the gaunt face stood there in the darkening evening holding his case. Then the blessed Mrs. Hudson came out. I was happier to see her than I had ever been to see anyone. There is a freshness about her that exists in no one else. Her rosy checks and clean apron always remind me of magnificent meals and clean sheets. She hugged me and turned to the tall gentleman to my left.

"Welcome home, sir. I hope your trip was useful."

"Indeed," said the rough voice, "but I never expected the USA would be so lucrative for my business interests. I am glad to be home, however. How are the boys and bees?"

"All is well here," she said, "and you must show the kind doctor around the premises as soon as the sunlight allows."

The boys were almost grown and quite handsome. I would have sworn they were young English lads except for the slight accents in their speech.

"Come," insisted Holmes, "it is time for drinks and roast prepared especially by Mrs. Hudson for this homecoming."

Mrs. Hudson had accompanied Holmes to the farm. She lost her husband earlier to some horrid debilitating disease. It was brave of her to relinquish her landlady duties to minister to Holmes, who as you know, can be difficult at times. The warm and cheery house offset the windy night.

Later, the wind from the Bay of Sussex howled, shaking the oaks about as we sat for an English dinner. The conversation was lively and intellectual. We all ate together including Mrs. Hudson and the gardener/chauffeur, Phillip, who also served as a tutor for the boys. After the dinner, the boys left to do their studies and puzzles and the three of us—Moriarty, myself and Holmes—sat by the fire. As a special treat for me, an ancient Calvados appeared.

"I promise you we will begin some explanation during our morning walk," said Holmes. "You will find it interesting for your writings."

Morning came and I looked from my window at the sun over the bay. I realized I needed the rest. Bianca had stayed in London for some time, but it didn't work out. She was interesting, but hardly intellectual. She returned to Paris and her previous position as a cabaret singer. I realized now how much I missed the comradery and intellectual conversations that seemed to follow Holmes.

I ate a full English breakfast prepared by the smiling Mrs. Hudson. There were no croissants or little cakes. My plate was filled with English ham, eggs, country bread and homemade jams accompanied by huge cups of fresh tea.

Then we began our walk down the path to the chalk hills over the bay.

"Now, my dear Watson, we will explain. As I told you, the characters you have written about were all children together in Dublin and we began our college studies together. They will always be a part of my life."

"Even Moriarty?" I asked.

"Of course," said Holmes. "The scenario begins as a wager when we were younger. The question was what behavior would lead to the greatest good in the world. Each of us would work from a different direction with the same goal—to eradicate evil. Sebastian, whom you must now recognize as a famous Irish writer, argued that the ways one lived one's life were enough. He was thwarted on all sides by those professing to understand morality, as memorized in the English churches and stuffy schools."

"And I believed in the power of money and big business," admitted Moriarty. "I am older and perhaps wiser now. We separated to meet our goals, but stayed true to our commitment and to each other. I was insanely jealous when Holmes and Sebastian renewed their friendship, but I did not know he was dying. In point, it may be Sebastian who wins the wager in the long run, at least after enough time has passed. We forgot, as optimistic young lads, the part time plays as a factor in bringing about our goals."

"A serious miscalculation on my part." said Holmes.

"Much of what you have seen involved interactive 'scare tactics and mirrors'," said Moriarty. "On the other hand, we were very competitive."

"Do you mean many of your cases were make-believe?" I asked.

"Of course not," said Holmes, "but we did perform a bit for the benefit of your reading public. Your stories were an impetus to keep the game going. In fact, our interactions at all levels led to our solving of many crimes, but we faked the dramatic at times. Let's use the last case as an example of our methodology, not the perfect example, but the one most fresh in our minds."

"Your current story began with our tussle over the falls," recalled Moriarty. "We did not fall into the water or anywhere. We made it seem that way to be more exiting in your public reader's eye."

Holmes continued the account, "The trip to Paris was a bit unplanned. We both needed to visit Sebastian, who was quite ill, and the thought of death brings old friends together. We did not predict that Franco would meet an unfortunate death, but we were already aware of the problem of the prostitution of the boys. We heard the story from Sebastian who was quite concerned."

"I left for Paris earlier to purchase the disreputable boys' house from Ramirez who needed money to pay his gambling debts." said Moriarty. "I allowed him and his brother to continue to their jobs since it gave us the chance to implicate them further. I even bought the circus. We will go to Paris again when it is in town. It no longer has debt-bound boys, believe me. Just for future reference in your writings, having adequate financial resources is beneficial in meeting one's goals."

"The perpetrators of this horrid scheme were stopped," said Holmes. "Each of us took a different path to get there, however."

"What then?"

"Ah," said Holmes, "this is our game. Each must outsmart the other in their solution."

"In the recent case, one could not predict the events." said Moriarty. "This was a sad case for me since I knew Franco well. By the way, I also know Bianca well. I am sorry things did not go perfectly for you, but I will tell you now Bianca was involved in the entire operation. It was one of the things that drove Franco to suicide. She left you and returned to Paris because she may be charged with her role in the crimes."

"Good heavens," I said. "I was duped."

"Perhaps. She is nice woman in her own peculiar way. I am sure she cared. Becoming judgmental is a waste of time which you can use for more valuable thoughts."

Holmes interjected, "Another example was in knowing the members of the freak show always came into the main building during their break. Once we knew there were probable witnesses, Moriarty used his position of the head of the circus to insist they tell all. I correctly determined the cause of death by deductive reasoning, but Moriarty proved this by being in a position of power. Now you will begin to see the game more clearly."

"But who won?" I asked.

"So, this one was a draw between us," said Holmes, "but there is an independent score keeper who will send us the outcome."

We returned to drinks. Moriarty was not the devil I thought, but rather a nice individual. He maintains numerous businesses and philanthropies, but they are legal. He paid for the rehabilitation of many of the rent boys.

For the rest of my stay, I learned more and more about each of their cases. I can only ask, dear reader, that you reread the stories in light of the new facts.

I left Sussex Downs by loud motorcar at Holmes insistence with a promise to return as soon as possible. I needed to attend to my medical practice to placate my patient patients. In the spring of 1904 I took the train back to Sussex.

I was offered the guest house and will run a smaller medical practice in Sussex. This will give me time revise my writings over the last 20 years, and also to rest and enjoy my life with Mrs. Hudson.

* * *

May 5, 1904
"Dear Dr. Watson,

You must leave the stories as they are.

By the way, I am the keeper of the game score.

Mycroft Holmes"

HOW LONG

Jennifer Maloney

At the coffee house on South, I wait for you
and she. I drink tea
made of sweet, red flowers and don't smoke
the cigarette I want to smoke
that I haven't smoked
in six years. It's been four months
and a new girl
since I've seen you.
Is that enough? Because,
I'll wait.

For four more months.
A year. Another girl or boy.
A pack of cigarettes. Another summer,
winter, spring
a novel, a new poem
a bowl of fruit.

I'll wait a wedding.
A birth.

I'll wait a war,
a pestilence, a new administration.

A sun
and a moon
and a long, rainy day.
A text message.
An email.

I'm not good at it.
But I'm practiced.
If you come tonight,

open the door, walk in,
pull out her chair.
Order a dirty chai and smile.

Sit down next to me.
Close enough to touch.
Like you're my friend.

My friend who taught me waiting
is nearly just the same as love. It's close enough.
Close enough to touch, as your fingers,
square-tipped and blunt as truth,
sweep across her face
like the hands of a clock,
caress her chin, kiss
the red flower of her mouth.

I turn my face toward the street.

Watch the unending stream of passing cars,
the ancient, burning stars
following their courses.
Down the block, a church bell chimes
and like all changeless things,
I wait.

AUTHOR ACKNOWLEDGMENTS

PIECING TOGETHER A FRACTURED LIFE:
A COMING OUT STORY (p. 189)

Robert Kenneth Anderson is a past winner of the Loft-McKnight creative nonfiction competition and a former S.A.S.E./Jerome Foundation fellow. In 2001 and 2006, he was awarded $1,000 prize for essays on blindness by VSA (Very special Arts) Minnesota, and in 2003 was named a winner of the Writers Rising Up essay competition. His poems and essays have appeared in numerous small publications, and in 2008 he self-published a memoir with Lulu.com: *Out of Denial: Piecing Together a Fractured Life*.

FOOTNOTES (p. 63)

Erin L. Cork writes fiction, non-fiction and poetry. She studied Creative Writing at the University of Montana. Her work has appeared in Quill Books. Her story *Knock, Knock* recently received Honorable Mention from *Glimmer Train*. Her first novel, *White Bread Twister* and short story collection *Hits and B-Sides* are forthcoming.

WAS GONE (p. 19)

Cirrus Julian is a Queer and non-binary student who studies creative writing at Oberlin College. They write a lot about bodies, and what it means to have a tangible body as a transgender person. They also like to write about space and flowers and love and other neat things.

ORIGINAL SIN (p. 33)

Stacey Darlington is a multi-published author of finely crafted lesbian fiction. Her novels both placed in The Rainbow Book Awards. She weaves her love for the supernatural, the occult and psychology into her work, making her stories thought-provoking and unique. Stacey writes and illustrates books for the junior audience, as well. Stacey lives in Florida.

LESBIANA (p. 149)

Erika De Jesus Rodriguez is a Latina performer, writer, dancer/model, photographer, and actress (mostly alone in her room, but sometimes on an actual stage). Growing up around performers it's no wonder she is in constant need of a spotlight. Erika is the co-creator of the bilingual poetry group named "Lingual." She considers Eduardo Galeano, Frida Kahlo and Carla Estrada her personal heroes (and jokingly, her grandparents). Catch her at on stage at various events throughout NY.

REVELATION (p. 165)

Jonathan Everitt has co-led a workshop for LGBTQ poets at Rochester's Out Alliance and co-hosts a monthly open mic at Equal Grounds coffeehouse in Rochester. Jonathan is currently an MFA candidate in creative writing at Bennington College. He lives in Webster, NY, with his partner, David Sullivan.

GIRL, YOU KNOW ITS TRUE COLORS (p. 167)

Allison Fradkin is a lipstick lesbian with thespian tendencies. Her work appears in *Upstaged: An Anthology of Queer Women and the Performing Arts*, *Through the Hourglass: An Anthology of Lesbian Historical Romance*, and *QDA: A Queer Disability Anthology*. To find the pot of lip gloss at the end of the rainbow, visit allisonfradkin.blogspot.com.

CHRYSALIS (p. 129)

Sam Gray is a queer non-binary trans-masculine poet from the Pittsburgh area who aims to reach the humanity in all people by writing openingly about the queer community. Sam is currently an undergraduate of English Literature and Gender Studies at Seton Hill University and was previously published in *Eye Contact*.

NUCLEAR FAMILIES (p. 139)

Youngest of 8 children, **Matt Hall** writes about his experiences of being gay in a non-affirming family. A graduate of UR (BA 2003, BCS & ASL) and UCSD (PhD 2012, Cognitive Psychology), he is now an assistant professor of Psychology at UMass-Dartmouth, living with his husband in Providence, RI.

SHERLOCK HOLMES AND THE CIRCUS (p. 225)

Adjie Henderson is a scientist and previously a Dean for Graduate Sciences. She has published over two hundred articles on scientific subjects and made numerous public and TV appearances related to science. More recently she has published short stories, none of which have to do with the credentials above.

FOSSIL FUELED (p. 187)

Aimee Herman is a Brooklyn-based queer writer and teacher with two full-length books of poetry including *meant to wake up feeling* (great weather for MEDIA) and *to go without blinking* (BlazeVOX books). Aimee plays ukulele/sings in the poetryband, Hydrogen Junkbox.

OTHER (p. 17)

Reilly Hirst is a poet, philosopher and activist. She (insert pronoun here) has been published in *Bitch Goddess*, *The Advocate*, academic journals, precedent-setting briefs, and is the food columnist for *The Empty Closet*. In her "spare" time, she writes and reads poetry, and gets out, like a lot.

A BLIZZARD OF SOLITUDE (p. 131)

J L Homan is retired and lives in western Massachusetts. He was the first member of either parents' families to achieve a college degree; enjoyed living twenty-seven years in Manhattan, during which he kicked his legs and sang his songs in three Broadway musicals as well as toured North America in several musical tours; was scholar-shipped with two international dance companies; survived the AIDS pandemic while sharing sixteen monogamous, mutually beneficial, loving and HIV-Negative years with a dear man who died of a Glioblastoma Multiformé (before either turned fifty years of age); and is attempting to rewrite the narrative of his life while dealing daily with the existential angst and irony that comes with growing older and learning to let go.

SMEAR THE QUEER (p. 71)

John Jeffire was born in Detroit. His novel *Motown Burning* won the 2005 Mount Arrowsmith Novel Competition and the 2007 Independent Publishing Awards Gold Medal for Regional Fiction. Former U.S. Poet Laureate Philip Levine called his first poetry collection, *Stone + Fist + Brick + Bone*, "a terrific one for our city." For more on the author and his work, visit writeondetroit.com.

CINDERELLA (p. 209)

Laurel Johanson is a Canadian LGBTQ+ writer from small-town Ontario now residing in Winnipeg, Manitoba. She is expected to graduate with a degree in Creative Communications from Winnipeg's Red River College in 2019, and is working toward publishing her first novel (LGBTQ+ themed) in the spring of 2019.

U'LL FEEL ME ALL AROUND U (p. 31)

Marissa Layne Johnson is a world-traveling, Beyonce-worshipping, wine-loving, gay woman living in Boston, Massachusetts. She is a poet, educator, and activist whose writing serves to break silences, call attention to social problems, and illuminate the complexity of human emotion, typically centered on survival, resilience, and emotional vulnerability.

A REAL LOVE (p. 141)

Sari Katharyn likes to write and wants to be a filmmaker. She has never been to a wedding. She would like her first to be a gay one. If you would like to invite her to yours, you can find her procrastinating on twitter @queer_sk.

ON JUDY GARLAND (p. 73)

Brian Kirst is a Chicago-based writer and freelance journalist. As the founder of *Big Gay Horror Fan*, he examines the world of horror through a queer perspective. His work has also appeared in the *Chicago Free Press*, the *Windy City Times* and other LGBTQ publications.

AT THE RED LIGHT, A MEMORY (p. 77)

Ben Kline lives in Cincinnati, Ohio, working at a library, drinking more coffee than seems wise. His work is forthcoming or has recently appeared in *The Offing, Bending Genres, Typehouse Magazine, Beech Street Review, The Matador Review, Impossible Archetype*, and many more. You can read more at https://benkline.tumblr.com/publications.

LET ME ASK YOU SOMETHING (p. 1)

Margaret H. Lange is a poet and lesbian living, working, and writing in Central Texas. Currently a graduate student and assistant youth services librarian, her past work includes retail and food service. Writing for more than a decade, Margaret is happiest when surrounded by books, cats, and air conditioning.

HOW LONG (p. 257)

Jennifer Maloney lives, writes and reads locally and parts east. Her work can be read in the *Poets Speak* anthology series published by Jules Poetry Playhouse and Beatlick Press, *A Flash of Dark, Volume 2*, edited by Scott W. Williams, and this year's edition of *Aaduna*, published by Bill Berry.

SHEATH! (p. 223)

Mary Panke lives near Hartford, CT with her family. Her work appears or is forthcoming in several journals including *Word Fountain*, *Poetry City, USA*, *Whale Road Review* and *Fredericksburg Literary & Art Review*. She is a 2017 Pushcart Poetry nominee.

FREDDIE AT THE BAR (p. 97)

Nicole Pergue received an MFA in poetry from Hunter College, where she was the recipient of the Mary M. Fay Award in Poetry. Her work has appeared in the online journal *Impossible Archetype* and *Brine Journal*. She is a native New Yorker from Queens. She can be reached at nicolepergue@gmail.com.

AN ENCOUNTER IN DOWNTOWN VANCOUVER, CANADA (p. 111)

Amanda Rodriguez is a queer, first-generation Cuban-American and environmentalist living in Weaverville, NC. Her writing can be found in *Germ Magazine*, *Pine Mountain Sand & Gravel*, *Mud Season Review*, *Thoughtful Dog*, *Rigorous*, *Stoneboat Literary Journal*, *Change Seven*, *Cold Creek Review*, *The Acentos Review*, *Label Me Latina/o*, and *Lou Lit Review*.

BEALTAINE (p. 61)

Anjuli Sherin is a Pakistani American feminist poet with a love of sensual language and eastern poetry forms. She focuses primarily on spirituality, nature, politics, love, and the human condition in her creative work, and writes poetry that is meant to be read out loud.

ON THE BRIDGE (p. 101)

Subraj Singh is a writer from Guyana. He was a Writer-in-Residence at the University of Iowa, and he's had fellowships from the International Writing Program and the Gabriel Garcia Marquez Foundation. His work has been published in *The Arts Journal*, *A World of Prose for CSEC*, and *Caribbean Beat*.

YOU CAME BACK (p. 151)

After retiring from full-time work, **David K. Slay** participated for two years in the UCLA Extension Writers' Program. He is interested in writing short literary fiction that can spark self-awareness within readers. His stories can be found in *Gold Man Review*, *Random Sam*ple, and elsewhere. He lives in Seal Beach, CA.

RAINI IS LUCA:
WHEN MY DAUGHTER BECAME MY SON (p. 7)

Shelley Stoehr is the author of four critically acclaimed YA novels. Recently, her work has appeared in *Fresh Ink, The Gordian Review,* and *Dead Alive Magazine.* She received an honorable mention in the 2017 Writer's Digest Annual Competition and was a runner-up in WOW! Women on Writing's flash fiction contest (2017). Her two children—Luca (ftm, age 17) and Ren (mtf, age 12) are transgender. Shelley is an MFA candidate at Southern CT State University, and an adjunct instructor of English.

CHANGING I'S (p. 79)

Jarred Thompson graduated from Alabama State University (Summa Cum Laude) in English. He then completed his Honours Degree in English (Cum Laude) at The University of Johannesburg in 2017. His poetry and fiction have been published in *Typecast Literary Magazine, Type House Literary Magazine* and *The Best New African Poets Anthology.*

NEVER, EVER BRING THIS UP AGAIN (p. 113)

After ten years as a filmmaker, **Randi Triant** received her MFA in writing and literature from Bennington College. Her fiction and nonfiction have appeared in literary journals and magazines. *The Treehouse* was published by Sapphire Books Publishing in 2018 and was called by Foreword Reviews an "insightful character-driven novel."

MAXINE WHO WAS ONCE MAX (p. 207)

Stephen Scott Whitaker (@SScottWhitaker) is a member of National Book Critics Circle and the managing editor for *The Broadkill Review.* His poems have appeared in *Oxford Poetry, Grub Street,* and *Anderbo,* among other journals. He is the author of three chapbooks, including the Dogfish Head Poetry Prize winning *Field Recordings,* and the USA Book Award nominee, *All My Rowdy Friends.*

EDITORIAL ACKNOWLEDGMENTS

READING PANEL VOLUNTEER

Frances Chang Andreu is a librarian at the Rochester Institute of Technology. She has a bachelor's in Creative Writing from Binghamton University, where she was an intern for the literary magazine, *Harpur Palate*. She also writes and draws comics on the side.

READING PANEL VOLUNTEER

Deanna Baker is a longtime ImageOut volunteer and an avid reader of both fiction and non-fiction. This project has inspired her to begin writing again after a long hiatus.

READING PANEL VOLUNTEER

Elizabeth Bell dreamed of becoming a doctor; however, girls were to become nurses who married doctors. She volunteered in the O.R., witnessed surgeries, transplants, amputations, changed her major, became an editorial assistant, professional dancer, walked across the USA, became a ranch hand, horse mid-wife, carpenter, pastor, retired to care for her mother and write.

READING PANEL VOLUNTEER

Nancy Brown is a first-time evaluator for *ImageOutWrite*. Long a fan of ImageOut, she's loved being a member of ImageOut's wonderful board for a number of years (she has a head for words, not a head for numbers).

READING PANEL VOLUNTEER

Ryan DeWolfe, English teacher of ten years for Geneva High School, is happy to help edit and evaluate *ImageOutWrite* again. He has been teaching AP Literature for over five years now and loves to dabble in his own creative writing. His favorite authors include Irving, Dickens, Chopin, and Wilde.

READING PANEL VOLUNTEER

Steve Farrington is a professor of French and Spanish at Monroe Community College who also holds a BA in English from SUNY Brockport. In his spare time, he loves traveling, reading, writing, learning languages, and running. He is the author of *Rodrigo's Land*, a novel of historical fiction.

READING PANEL VOLUNTEER

Rochester, NY, native **Judy Fuller** has been writing poetry since she was five. An Anglophile, she spent a college year in England and a Fulbright year in Scotland. She teaches at Quest elementary in Hilton, NY, and helps her husband run Simply New York Marketplace & Gifts in Irondequoit, NY.

READING PANEL VOLUNTEER

Gregory Gerard's work has been published by *Tiny Lights, Jonathan, Lake Affect*, and more. He teaches writing part-time at Writers & Books, Rochester NY's contemporary literary center. Gerard is the author of the gay memoir *In Jupiter's Shadow*, editor of *The Big Brick Review*, and very honored to be the past editor of *ImageOutWrite Vols. 5&6*. Visit him online at www.gregorygerard.net.

EDITOR

Jessica Heatly is a professional ghostwriter and content marketing consultant. Her personal work appears in projects such as this, and on blogs celebrating topics like pinball, Rochester, LGBTQ+ life, and adventure travel.

COVER ARTIST

Lola Flash uses photography to challenge stereotypes and offer new ways of seeing that transcend and interrogate gender, sexual, and racial norms. She received her bachelor's degree from Maryland Institute and her Masters from London College of Printing, in the UK. Flash works primarily in portraiture with a 4x5 film camera, engaging those who are often deemed invisible. In 2008, she was a resident at Lightwork. Most recently, Flash was awarded an Art Matters grant, which allowed her to further two projects, in Brazil and London. Flash has work included in important public collections such as the Victoria and Albert Museum in London. Her work is featured in the publication *Posing Beauty*, edited by Deb Willis, currently on exhibit across the US, and she is in the current award-winning film *Through a Lens Darkly*. Flash's work welcomes audiences who are willing to not only look but see.